He took a deep breath.

"All right, I'm going to do one of two things. Either I'm going to kiss you, or you're going to tell me to leave now, and I won't see you again."

She stared at him.

"Sadie?"

"I. . ."

"It's up to you."

"I don't want you to leave, but—"

Harry didn't wait for her to finish. He drew her up out of her chair, and his lips found hers. Sadie tensed for an instant. Had she given the wrong answer?

No, her heart told her. *You love him. This is the right thing.*

She let him draw her closer, reveling in the joy his touch brought her. It was far beyond her expectations or imaginations, and she wanted the moment to last forever. He held her in his arms and showered soft kisses along her temple, to the corner of her eye.

"Sadie, I love you so much."

She gulped for air, knowing that all she needed to say was two words: *Don't leave.*

And then what? Would he be embroiled in their troubles, too? Or would he betray them when he found out the truth? The joy that had flooded her a moment ago was overcome by guilt, and she pushed him away reluctantly.

SUSAN PAGE DAVIS and her husband, Jim, have been married thirty years and have six children, ages twelve to twenty-eight. They live in Maine, where they are active in an independent Baptist church. Susan is a homeschooling mother and news writer. She has published short stories in the romance, humor, and mystery fields. Her books include historical romance, mystery, and children's fantasy.

Books by Susan Page Davis

HEARTSONG PRESENTS
HP607—Protecting Amy
HP692—Oregon Escort
HP708—The Prisoner's Wife

Weaving a Future

Susan Page Davis

Heartsong Presents

To our second daughter, Megan, an author in her own right, who is brave enough to critique her mom's work. I can't wait to see our joint byline!

A note from the Author:
I love to hear from my readers! You may correspond with me by writing:

Susan Page Davis
Author Relations
PO Box 721
Uhrichsville, OH 44683

ISBN 1-59789-058-8

WEAVING A FUTURE

Our mission is to publish and distribute inspirational products offering exceptional value and biblical encouragement to the masses.

PRINTED IN THE U.S.A.

one

May, 1848

Harry had never seen such fine country for horses. He had to admit, this Shenandoah Valley rivaled the rolling hills in Kentucky where he planned to set up his breeding farm. The meadows burst with a green opulence in the May sun. The grass grew so lush he was tempted to get down and roll in it and to take Pepper's saddle off and let him roll in it, too.

They trotted along a fencerow, and a half-dozen mares tore across the pasture toward them. They kept pace with Pepper as they strode along inside the rail fence, snorting and nickering, trying to capture Pepper's attention. The gelding snuffled and tossed his head but kept on steadily under Harry's firm hand. Every mare had a long-legged foal at her side, he noted. It would have been hard to choose among them for the best.

On Harry's left, a hardwood forest fringed the road. The oaks and hickories, in their full, glorious foliage, would offer some shade on that side of the lane in the morning; but now it was late afternoon, and the warmth of the golden rays striking him from the west, beyond the meadows and more rolling hills, was not unpleasant.

He heard muffled hoofbeats and turned toward the woods. Two horses charged neck-and-neck from a shady path and bolted into the lane in front of him. Pepper reared with an alarmed squeal as a bay mare rushed toward him. Harry's instantaneous impression of the rider was a young woman gone wild. Her features were lovely, lit with the joy of speed. As he jerked Pepper's reins she caught sight of him, and shock darkened her eyes as she realized the inevitability of the coming collision.

"Whoa!" She pulled back with all her strength, gritting her teeth in determination. Harry pivoted Pepper on his hind legs, attempting to lessen the impact.

He had no time to do more. In a split second her mare slammed against Pepper's hindquarters, sending the gelding in an awkward leap toward the pasture fence. Harry watched in dismay while trying to keep his balance. As she flew from the saddle, the girl's commodious burgundy skirts billowed with air, like the sails of the schooner Harry had called his home for the last three years. As she tumbled to earth, he had a glimpse of lace-trimmed linen and high black boots. Her bay mare veered to the left with an offended snort and skittered up the lane.

"Miss Sadie!" Beyond the fallen girl, a thin Negro boy was pulling up his own mount, a red roan, and staring with horror at the girl. At least he'd been riding on her other side and had avoided becoming part of the melee. Pepper lurched and snorted, but Harry held his head down, and the gelding halted, calming under the soft words Harry spoke in his ear.

He and the boy leaped to the ground at the same moment, and they knelt, one on either side of the girl. She lay on her back, staring up at them, breathing in quick, shallow gasps. Her blue eyes sought Harry's face in confusion. Her auburn hair was no doubt confined in a sedate knot at ordinary times, but now a long braid trailed in the dirt by her shoulder, and fine wisps fanned out around her face.

"Miss Sadie, you done what your papa said and broke your neck!" Tears streamed down the boy's face as he leaned within inches of her nose. "Tell me you ain't broke your neck, Miss Sadie!"

"Hush, Pax!" The girl hauled in a longer, slower breath and exhaled carefully. "I think I'll live, if you'll give me some air."

"Take it easy," Harry said. "Get your breath back."

"The horses." She struggled to sit up, swiveling to look.

The bay mare had disappeared around a bend in the lane, and Pax's roan was snatching mouthfuls of grass at the edge of the road. The girl moaned and lay back gasping, putting one hand up to her head. "Get Lily."

"You sure you all right?" the boy asked uneasily.

"I'll be fine. Just get that horse!" She took several more shallow gulps and gasped, "If she gets back home without me, Papa will never let me ride again!"

The boy jumped up and ran to his mount. He scooped up the trailing reins and hopped into the saddle then tore off in the direction the bay had taken.

Harry watched the girl, waiting patiently for her to recover. She was older than he'd first thought—a young lady, of that he was certain from her clothing and her manner with the Negro boy. Probably the daughter of a planter. Her disinclination to swoon or cry assured him she had taken tumbles before and was not seriously injured. He was sure her corset was obstructing her breathing. Not much he could do about that.

She lay quiet for nearly a minute, her head turned away from him, gradually gaining control of her breath. At last she turned slowly toward him.

"May I help you up, ma'am?"

He read speculation, embarrassment, and something more in her blue eyes before the lids flickered down to conceal them.

"I don't believe I've ever laid eyes on you before in my life, sir."

Harry laughed. "I beg your pardon, miss. I should have introduced myself. My name is Harry Cooper."

"Cooper?" She sat up with a little moan, and Harry touched her shoulder gently.

"Are you certain you're not hurt?"

She rubbed her elbow then flexed her arm, frowning at the cuff of her dress where a button had been scraped off. "I'll be fine, thank you." She glanced up at him, wincing. "I've made rather a spectacle of myself, haven't I? I apologize, sir."

"No need, although spirited horses and daredevil riders can

be a volatile combination."

She blinked once then smiled. "Indeed. It was a race."

"A very close one, I'd say."

"I'd have won if you hadn't been in the way."

Harry couldn't help smiling. "Are you sure? Those horses were pretty evenly matched."

Her cheeks colored slightly, and she looked away, but the smile didn't leave her lips. "Here comes Pax."

Harry bit back his disappointment at seeing the boy returning on his roan, leading the young woman's mare. She gathered herself to rise, and he slipped his hand under her uninjured elbow to give her a hint of leverage.

"I thank you for your concern," she said, facing him as she brushed a fine cloud of powdery dirt from her skirt. "Your horse wasn't injured, was he?"

"No, he's fine, ma'am. Allow me to see you home." His quick offer surprised him a little. He wasn't used to playing the gallant gentleman, but something about this untamed beauty drew him like north drew the needle on the captain's compass.

"No need, I assure you." Her breath came easier now but was still a bit choppy.

Harry looked the two mares over. Their conformation was nearly perfect, and both were walking sedately now, scarcely breathing hard.

The boy rode up close to where Harry and the young woman stood and halted, swinging down to the ground. "Lemme help you up, Miss Sadie."

Harry sensed the boy's mistrust directed at him, but he was no doubt the guardian for this lovely young woman and was privileged to ride his master's best mounts when the daughter of the house went out for exercise.

"The horses seem none the worse for the accident," Harry said.

"Yes. I thank you for your help." She stepped toward the bay, where Pax stood waiting to aid her. Harry knew he could easily pick her up in his arms and place her in the saddle.

Better belay that idea, he told himself. He was certain Miss Sadie and the fiercely scowling Pax would never allow it. She was about to leave him, a cheerless thought that set Harry to wondering how he could draw out the encounter without offending her. But she was astride now, settling her voluminous skirt around her with a couple of gentle strokes and gathering her reins.

She's left her hoops home, Harry thought with a wry smile. *She must be near twenty, but she has a child's unconscious freedom.* Her energy and boldness, coupled with a resolve to act the proper lady under the gaze of a stranger, made him envy Pax. *I wouldn't mind riding beside her day after day.*

"Good day then, sir." She turned and headed away, down the lane, and the boy scrambled aboard his mare.

"Wait!" Harry called. Pax looked back uncertainly, but the young woman kept her mare at a steady walk away from him.

"I'm looking for the Spinning Wheel Farm, owned by Mr. Oliver McEwan," Harry said to the boy.

Pax grinned. "This be your lucky day, suh. You done found it."

Harry was startled at how quickly the boy's animosity turned to welcome. "You mean this is McEwan land?"

The boy gestured to the fields on the other side of the lane. "Everythin' you see, suh."

"And the house?"

"Yonder." He nodded after the girl's retreating figure.

"Thank you." Harry stroked Pepper's neck and watched them ride out of sight before he mounted. He let Pepper amble along in the golden light of sunset. Beautiful country, absolutely gorgeous. There couldn't be two farms with such superb animals in the area. Did he dare hope he would once more meet the lovely young Sadie, who strove with marginal success to cloak her effervescence in propriety? He smiled to himself, remembering the quality of the horses Sadie and her faithful companion rode. Yes, he dared hope.

two

Sadie donned a huge apron and tied the strings behind her. She loved the kitchen, with the savory smell of roasting poultry and the warmth of the cookstove. When she wasn't out feeding the chickens or in the barn coddling the horses, she spent many contented hours here with Tallie, the family's cook and housekeeper.

Tallie threw her an ominous frown. "You just get into the parlor and help your father entertain the gentleman."

"Don't fuss at me," Sadie said. "I always help you with supper. Papa's perfectly capable of keeping up a conversation with a customer."

"Hmm." Tallie plucked her green-handled masher from a nail on the wall over her worktable and plunged it into a pan of boiled potatoes. As she worked with strong, methodical strokes, she scowled at Sadie. "It's *dinner* tonight, served in the dinin' room, and I can fix it. Now that you're all cleaned up and lookin' respectable, you belong in there with the company."

"He'll see me soon enough." Sadie began arranging Tallie's golden biscuits on an ironstone platter.

"Pax said that gentleman was taken with you, though I don't know why, with you dashin' 'round the country like a hoyden." Tallie turned her brown eyes heavenward in despair. "I don't know how to keep you from shamin' this family, Miss Sadie."

"Now, you hush. Don't you dare tell Papa I fell off Lily this afternoon."

"It's a wonder you didn't meet your end." Tallie sighed, reaching for the butter. "And that dress you wore is near done for, I'll tell you!"

Sadie lifted the platter of biscuits and turned sideways, allowing her full hoopskirt to slide through the doorway to the dining room. She placed the platter on the table and tiptoed to the door on the far side of the room. When she held her breath, she could hear her father's warm voice coming from the parlor.

"You want six mares, Mr. Cooper? I'll have to think on that. Don't want to deplete my own herd too much. I can let you have four with no problem."

"Four will be a good start," Cooper said.

Her father went on. "If it's breeding stock you want, the sorrel is a good choice. She's dropped two good foals. And any of the others I showed you. Of course, I don't like to let my mares go until their foals are weaned."

Good! Sadie thought. *He's going to buy, and we'll have some money at last.* Her father had been short on cash this spring.

"Well, sir, I can come back in the fall if you'd like," Harry Cooper was saying. "I've picked out my property in Kentucky, but I haven't started building yet. I've got my summer's work cut out for me."

"It's a long ride," Oliver McEwan said.

"Not too far, sir, and I'd like to see this valley in the fall."

At that moment Tallie entered from the kitchen, holding a big porcelain tureen full of potatoes. "What you doin'?" she hissed, and Sadie straightened and pulled away from the doorway.

"Mr. Cooper's going to buy some horses from Papa," Sadie whispered.

Tallie smiled with satisfaction. "Isn't that fine? Now you get in there. Everythin's ready, and I don't want your papa waitin' on you until the biscuits get cold."

Sadie started to protest, but Tallie put her hands on her ample hips. "Git, git, git!"

Sadie could see she would have to do as she was told, and

she reached behind her to untie her apron.

Tallie's eyes lit with admiration. "You gonna break that poor man's heart, sugar. That dress makes you look like a princess."

Sadie looked down at the rose silk gown. She didn't have many occasions to dress up anymore. Her father hadn't entertained much since her mother's death four years ago. Occasionally a neighbor would invite them to dinner. She hoped suddenly that her dress was still fashionable and that she would compare favorably to the other ladies Harry Cooper had seen in his travels. Her meeting with him had been so brief that she wasn't certain whether he was a courteous gentleman or a presumptuous bounder. She hoped her father liked him. That would tell her a lot.

She stepped toward Tallie and planted a kiss soundly on her plump, dark cheek. Then she took a deep breath and headed for the parlor.

Her father was standing near the fireplace with Harry, holding the small daguerreotype of Sadie's brother, Tenley. Sadie paused in the doorway. How well she knew that picture! Tenley stood stiff and proud in his dark forage cap and the white cotton uniform of the Second Dragoons. His eagerness and optimism glowed in his eyes.

"The boy's been gone a long time," her father was saying. "He wanted to go with General Taylor and whip those Mexicans. But it's been almost a year since we've heard from him."

"He's a fine lad," Harry said. "I'm sure you'll hear something soon."

"I hope so. We pray for him constantly. My solace is knowing he's in God's hands."

Harry nodded. "If your son is trusting the Lord, you know he'll be all right, sir, no matter what happens. But our troops took the capital last fall. I expect he's on his way home now."

"Maybe." Her father placed the frame back on the mantelpiece, and Sadie stepped forward. Her skirt rustled, and her father turned toward her. "Ah, here she is at last. Mr. Cooper, I'd like you to meet my daughter, Sadie."

She half expected the guest to laugh and accuse her of masquerading as a lady or at least to announce that they had met before, but Harry's expression turned serious as he took her hand and bowed over it.

"Miss McEwan," he murmured. "This is a pleasure."

A thrill of anticipation tickled Sadie's spine. Her dread had been for nothing. This dinner could turn out to be pleasant indeed, if Harry Cooper decided to make it so.

"Sadie, our guest is buying some mares from us. He'll come back for them in September."

"That's wonderful. I'm sure you'll be pleased with them." She didn't quite dare look at Harry again. She was grateful that he apparently hadn't spilled the tale of her breakneck ride to her father. For a fleeting instant she thought, *Maybe he doesn't recognize me! I must have looked like an ill-bred roughneck when I crashed into him.*

But a quick glance at him from beneath her eyelashes disabused her of that notion. A secret laugh danced in Harry's rich brown eyes.

"Come then," her father said, offering Sadie his arm. "I'm sure Tallie is beside herself, wondering how to keep the food warm."

During the meal Tallie and her husband, Zeke, served them with flawless precision. Harry Cooper was polite and carried on an animated conversation about horses, farm land, and politics, though he claimed to know nothing about the latter topic, having spent the last three years at sea.

"At sea?" his host asked. "Where did you sail to?"

Harry sat back with a little sigh and let Zeke take away his dishes from the main course. "The Caribbean mostly, sir. We made several runs to the islands—Tortola, Antigua, Trinidad. . . ."

"Trinidad," Sadie whispered, rolling the sound off her tongue.

Harry smiled at her. "We put in at Caracas twice. Went out to the Spice Islands one time. It's beautiful, but it's not home."

Her father nodded. "So you've had enough of the sea?"

"Yes, sir. The captain of the vessel I shipped on decided to do a transatlantic voyage, and I knew I didn't want to go along."

"Rum?"

"Yes, sir."

Tallie came from the kitchen at that moment, carrying a huge, white-frosted layer cake, and Zeke followed, bearing two golden fruit pies, still warm from the oven.

"Oh, my." Harry retrieved his napkin from the tablecloth and spread it in his lap again.

"We're blessed with a wonderful cook," her father said.

Tallie beamed at him. "Bless you, Mr. Oliver."

Sadie intercepted Harry's look of mild surprise and smiled at him. He smiled back, and she felt her face go crimson as Tallie handed her a small porcelain plate with a slice of layer cake.

"So, Mr. Cooper, you'll be returning to Kentucky soon to start construction?" her father asked.

"Yes. I'll put up the barn first, sir."

"And why did you come all this way to buy your foundation stock?"

Harry smiled. "There aren't many farms well established in Kentucky yet, but it's growing. I was raised near Williamsburg and thought perhaps I'd go there for horses, but when I set out, people kept telling me to go to the Shenandoah Valley."

"Can't beat this country for raising horses, and that's a fact." Sadie's father lifted his fork and surveyed his peach pie.

"Yes, sir. It's a beautiful place, all right. And the closer I got, the harder I prayed."

Sadie waited eagerly to hear what he would say next.

"What was your prayer?" her father asked.

"I asked the Lord to show me where to find the best horses. And the closer I got, the more I heard the name McEwan."

Her father's smile was the brightest Sadie had seen it since her mother's death. She eyed Harry, hoping he was sincere, not just trying to gain favor with his host.

"The last three places I stopped, folks pointed up the valley and said I couldn't do better than here, sir."

"Well, now." Her father gestured to Zeke to bring him more tea.

Their talk went on, and Sadie was glad to be a spectator. Occasionally one of the men would ask her a question, and she would answer quietly, but most of the time she sipped her tea and covertly watched Harry Cooper. She noticed many things: his strong, tanned hands; his direct, respectful gaze into her father's face when listening to him; a small, faint scar over the corner of his right eye; and a decidedly rebellious lock of dark hair that fell onto his forehead. He was the most personable and handsome horse buyer her father had ever entertained.

When Zeke and Tallie left the room, Oliver McEwan turned to the guest. "Zeke has been with our family a long time. My grandfather freed his father and six other slaves he'd maintained. Most of them scattered, but Zeke's father stayed on with us. Zeke and I are about the same age, and we were almost like brothers."

"And Tallie?"

He shook his head. "I had to buy her from a neighbor. It was the only way Zeke could marry her. I gave Tallie her papers nigh twenty years ago. Their children are free."

"I admire you, sir."

Her father ducked his head. "It's not such a big thing, but in my opinion it's the right thing. Of course, not everyone in these parts agrees with me."

"I understand."

He smiled. "It's getting dark, Mr. Cooper. You must stay the night."

"Oh, no, I couldn't, sir. It's only five miles back to the village."

"I insist." Her father rose, his decision made. "I've already spoken to Tallie about my son's room. I think you'll be comfortable there."

Harry hesitated a moment and glanced toward Sadie.

Her father said, "We'll be able to continue our pleasant conversation, and perhaps my daughter will show you her mother's watercolors. My wife was quite an artist."

Sadie stared at him. "Really, Father—"

"I'd love to see them, Miss McEwan."

How could she refuse his inviting smile? She walked with Harry into the parlor, behind her father. With every step, she was conscious of his nearness. He waited for her to compress her crinoline and pass through the doorway. Sadie felt her color rise again. She wished this ungainly style would go out of fashion.

As her father settled into his favorite chair, she led Harry to the far wall where her favorite painting hung between two windows. "That's my brother, Tenley, when he was about eight. It's a good likeness."

Harry studied the watercolor of the boy walking a rail fence, his arms outstretched to balance him. "It's unusual. So informal. I like it."

Sadie smiled at him then, not holding back what she felt. "Mother usually painted landscapes, like that one over the mantel." She nodded toward it, and Harry turned to look. It was the same view the McEwans had from their veranda, the sloping meadows in the pastel greens of spring rolling to meet the dark mountains in the distance. "But I like this one of Tenley."

Harry nodded. "It captures his temperament, does it?"

"Yes. He's idealistic and imaginative, but. . ." She hesitated, alarmed to find tears springing into her eyes. "His faith is strong," she whispered.

Harry leaned toward her and said softly, "You miss him."

"Terribly."

He looked at the painting again. "I'll pray for him, if you don't think it presumptuous."

"Of course not. Thank you."

Sadie found that she couldn't look into his eyes any longer. They were too intent. She glanced at her father, but he had taken out his pocket watch and was winding it.

"You don't mind me staying in Tenley's room?"

"Of course not," she said.

"I won't disturb his things." Harry was watching her again, with those expressive brown eyes. A vision of a possible future came unbidden to Sadie's active mind. Beautiful horses; children with dark, wavy hair; and Harry Cooper.

"Do you care for a game of dominoes?" Her father's voice drew her back to reality.

She would have declined, but Harry said quickly, "That would be a pleasure, if Miss Sadie would join us."

She gulped. "All right." It meant she would have to sit beside him for another hour and try to keep from staring at him. But she knew it wouldn't be torture.

Her father rose and went to the doorway. "Zeke! Zeke!"

Harry leaned close to Sadie's ear. "That gown suits you admirably, Miss McEwan. I've been thinking it all evening and wishing I'd have a chance to say so."

Sadie's heart raced, and she couldn't help giving him a slight smile, but she felt it only proper to take a small step backward before her father turned toward them again.

three

Sadie couldn't help stroking the lush fabric as she spread out the end of the bolt to show her friend, Elizabeth Thurber.

Elizabeth sighed. "It's lovely."

"That green velvet is beautiful, Sadie," said Elizabeth's mother, Mary Thurber. "It would make Elizabeth look sallow, but you can wear it, my dear."

"I'm glad you didn't choose lavender," Elizabeth agreed. "You can wear bright colors with your complexion, and you should."

Tallie set the porcelain teapot down on the cherry table beside Sadie's chair. "That velvet gonna make her look like Queen Victoria's little sister." She smiled at Sadie and nodded toward the teapot. "You pour for the ladies now, Miss Sadie."

"Thank you, Tallie." Sadie reached for one of the thin china cups her mother had prized. Tallie had outdone herself with the tea tray today. She had artistically arranged wafer-thin sugar cookies and tiny butter tarts on the painted Italian charger Sadie's parents had received as a wedding gift more than twenty years ago. Small clusters of grapes were mounded in a cut-glass bowl. In spite of the warmth of the July afternoon, the tea was piping hot, served with honey, sugar, and cream.

Tallie smiled at Sadie and glided backward through the door, heading for her kitchen domain.

Mrs. Thurber accepted her cup of tea graciously but frowned slightly as Sadie began to pour a cup for Elizabeth.

"You're entirely too free with your help, Sadie, dear."

Sadie stared at her in momentary confusion. "But. . .Tallie

is my friend, Mrs. Thurber. And she's a free woman."

"Yes, child." The older woman sipped delicately from her cup then blotted her lips with a linen napkin. "Still, I'm certain your mother wouldn't be quite so familiar with the servants."

Sadie thought about that as she passed the cup to Elizabeth. Tallie was no different in her manner from how she had been when Mother was alive, was she? She had always been loving toward Sadie and outspoken in her opinions.

"Thank you," Elizabeth murmured with a smile, taking the cup and saucer.

Sadie then passed the platter of sweets, and Mrs. Thurber selected a cookie and a tart. "Your Tallie certainly can cook, I'll give her that."

"Yes, she's a treasure." Sadie offered the charger to Elizabeth.

"I suppose you can put up with a lot in return for her skills," Mrs. Thurber went on, "but you must never let them get insolent, my dear." She bit into the flaky tart and closed her eyes for a moment in pure bliss. "Delicious."

A quick retort was on the tip of Sadie's tongue, but she swallowed it, along with a gulp of tea. Her mother had trained her to be courteous, and her father had warned her before to keep peace with the ladies in the neighborhood. *You'll need your neighbors one day, Sadie. Don't make yourself odious to them now, no matter how insipid you find them. Their good opinion will stand you in good stead when hard times come.*

Sadie wasn't sure about that, but her love for her father made her keep silent, even though Mrs. Thurber's comments about Tallie seemed unjust. Tallie had been mother and mentor to her for the past four years, since her own dear mother's death.

"The pattern for the walking dress will look lovely in that ice blue muslin," Elizabeth offered, and Sadie smiled on her with gratitude for gently turning the conversation.

"Thank you so much for letting me borrow all your patterns."

"Anytime," Elizabeth assured her.

"That velvet is perfect for the evening dress," Mrs. Thurber said with a pert nod. "Although you may need to adjust the bodice a little. The neckline is a bit low for our country dinners. Of course, for Elizabeth's Richmond gowns we've gone with the fashions."

Elizabeth's cheeks colored slightly. "I'm having three new day dresses and two evening gowns made," she told Sadie with an air of confession. "Father is all the time complaining about the cost, but Mother says I shall need them."

"Oh, yes, those and more, most likely." Mrs. Thurber waved her hand before her. "We plan to spend several months in Richmond, you know."

"So Elizabeth told me."

"It's a pity you have no one in the city now," Elizabeth said.

Sadie nodded. "My aunt Thompson would have invited me, I'm sure, but her health is so poor now that she keeps to her home by the sea."

"That lovely green velvet will be wasted here." Elizabeth giggled. "There are no eligible men in the neighborhood. Unless you count the Kauffman boys, of course."

Sadie returned her grimace, and they both laughed.

"You should come with us," Mrs. Thurber said, and Sadie stared at her in shock.

"Oh, I couldn't. Father needs me. I help him a lot with the business now, you know."

"Nonsense. You oughtn't to be tearing about the countryside on horseback the way you do, Sadie. It's time you were settled." Mrs. Thurber stirred her tea pensively. "And you don't even have a proper riding habit. Yes, I think I shall speak to your father. You ought to have some time in town. It will give you polish."

Sadie felt a sudden panic. "Oh, but I couldn't go in September."

"Why ever not?"

"We expect guests." She felt her cheeks going crimson. After all, Harry Cooper wasn't exactly a guest, but she wouldn't leave the Shenandoah Valley for the world now, not with Harry coming back in a matter of weeks. "And Father has several buyers coming. He'll need me here to entertain for him."

"My, my, entertaining your father's business clients," Elizabeth said.

"Yes, well, they often take luncheon or dinner with us after talking business with Father."

"Then you must have a suitable wardrobe." Mrs. Thurber held out her cup, and Sadie refilled it. "Is Tallie as handy with a needle as she is at the stove?"

"She's quite good," Sadie said. "Mostly she helps me cut out my dresses and stitch the seams and hems. I do the embellishments. My mother taught me, you know."

"Yes, she was a marvelous seamstress. No one can match her beadwork."

"Do you ever wear any of your mother's dresses?" Elizabeth asked.

Sadie lowered her gaze. "Well, no, I don't expect they would fit me right."

Mrs. Thurber eyed her figure without pretense. "Yes, you've grown a lot this last year. You might even be taller than your mother was. You're a might thin yet, but I suppose you could take in the seams." She nodded. "Those lovely fabrics she wore. You ought to consider it."

"It would save your father piles of money," Elizabeth said.

Sadie swallowed hard. She had tried several times to sort through her mother's things, but every time she opened the wardrobe, she found herself crying. Tallie had assured her she could take her time in deciding what to do with her mother's clothes.

"I recall the dress she wore to my husband's birthday dinner the year before she passed on." Mrs. Thurber's eyes were focused on something beyond the parlor walls. "It was exquisite. White tulle with Chantilly lace. A frothy confection, but she carried it off." She looked at Sadie with a bittersweet smile. "Your mother was stunning. I always envied her complexion. And now you have it."

Elizabeth scowled. "I pop out in freckles if I get the least bit of sun."

Mrs. Thurber remained in the nostalgic mode. "Do you still have the old spinning wheel?"

Sadie nodded. "Yes, Father was going to get rid of it, but I asked him if I could have it as a keepsake. It's in my bedroom upstairs."

"I recall your grandmother spinning in this very room." Mrs. Thurber's gray eyes went all dreamy again. "Her hands were never idle, even while she visited with company. She used to make the finest wool yarns in the county. She gave me enough for a pair of hose one year as a birthday gift. Softer, neater hosiery I never saw."

An hour later, when her guests had gone, Sadie changed into her plain gray housedress. Before going down to the kitchen, she paused before the mirror in her bedroom and put her hand up to her cheek. Did she look like her mother? She hoped so. She was glad she had listened to Tallie and worn her bonnet faithfully this summer whenever she went out to ride. Would Harry find her attractive? She thought he had last May. Of course, any number of things might have transpired in Harry Cooper's life this summer. He might even have found himself a wife in Kentucky.

She hurried downstairs. Tallie was sliding the roasting pan into the oven, laden with half a plump ham.

"Your papa's home from town," Tallie said as Sadie reached for her apron.

"Oh, good! I hope he found the notions I asked him to get."

Tallie wiped her hands on her calico apron. "You gave Mr. Oliver a list, and if MacPheters's store had it, he bought it. You can count on that."

Sadie smiled and reached for the everyday ironstone plates. She took a stack of five from the shelf and began arranging them on the broad kitchen table.

"What are you doin'?" Tallie asked sharply.

"Father and I can eat in the kitchen with your family."

"It ain't proper." Tallie frowned and shook her head. "You and Mr. Oliver need to eat in the dinin' room, like gentlefolks."

"That's so silly. We're all friends. You and Zeke happen to work for my father, that's all."

"No, that's not all, and you know it. What if those fine Thurber ladies showed up while you was eatin' in the kitchen? The news would be all over this county by the weekend."

Sadie laughed and started to renew her protest, but Tallie placed her hands firmly on her hips and scowled at her. "You mind me now, Miss Sadie."

"But I often eat out here with you and Pax and—"

"I been too lax with you, that's for sure. What would your mama say? Besides, what if Mr. Cooper came in the middle of dinner? Hmm? You just put two of them plates back and put the good china on for you and your papa, in there." She pointed toward the dining room door with a stern look that left no room for argument. "Your papa wants you to turn out a lady, just like your mama was, and that's a fact."

Sadie sighed and picked up two of the plain white plates. She replaced them on the shelf and headed for the doorway. Her mother's best china was kept in a cabinet in the dining room.

"You do think he'll come back, don't you?" Immediately she

wished she hadn't asked. She'd tried so hard not to show how eagerly she awaited Harry's return, but what use was it? Tallie knew her so well that it was probably no secret.

Tallie smiled as she opened the flour bin. "He'll be back for certain. That man prayed to God, just like Abraham's servant, and God brought him here for a reason."

Sadie couldn't hold in the shy smile that pulled at her lips. "Do you think I'm that reason, Tallie?"

"Well, you just don't know, do you? Not only that, but he gave your papa half the money for them horses he's buyin'. He won't forget his unfinished business."

"I suppose you're right." Sadie pushed the door open with her hip. She set the table carefully for two, waiting for the heat to leave her cheeks before she rejoined Tallie in the kitchen. When she returned, Pax was coming in through the back door.

"Mr. Oliver say he'll be up to talk with Miss Sadie, soon as he and Pa take care of the horses."

"All right." Sadie wondered what lay behind this odd bit of news. It sounded as though her father had something special to discuss with her. Perhaps he hadn't been able to fill her list of sewing notions, after all. "Do you know if he got the things I asked for?"

Pax shrugged. "First we took the colt to Mr. Glassbrenner. Then he and Mr. Oliver went to the bank together."

"Good! That means he paid Papa in cash, and we're solvent again." Sadie grinned, but Pax's smooth face still held a worried look. "What is it?"

"Well. . .we went over to the store, and Mr. Oliver gave Mr. MacPheters his list. Then Mr. MacPheters gave him the mail, and Mr. Oliver started reading it while they got his goods for him."

Sadie watched him closely, wondering where this rambling tale was headed.

"Spit it out," Tallie chided, and Pax glanced at her then down at the floor.

"Then Mr. Oliver told me to bring everythin' out to the wagon, and he went outside."

Sadie stepped over close to Pax. The boy had been like a little brother to her—a pesky, troublesome little brother at times, and they didn't stand on ceremony with one another.

"Pax, you just tell me what's going on right now, or I'll box your ears."

"Me, too," Tallie said ominously.

Pax looked from Sadie to his mother then stepped back toward the door. "Ain't nothin' goin' on that I know of, except Mr. Oliver didn't speak to me after that, except to ask if I was sure I got everythin'."

Pax sidled toward the door, not looking at her, and Sadie reached out and grabbed the collar of his shirt. "You're not going anywhere."

"That's all I know, Miss Sadie. Honest."

She looked deep into his dark eyes then released her hold on him. "Fine. I'll find out soon enough anyway. Just you be ready to ride tomorrow before breakfast, you hear me?"

Pax grinned. "I be ready right after I milk the cow, Miss Sadie, unless your papa tells me to do somethin' else for him."

She nodded curtly and turned away. She hadn't ridden for a week, and she missed the long rambles with Pax. The heat had been overpowering throughout July, and her father and Tallie had both advised her to stay out of the sun. But enough was enough, so she had made a date with Pax to ride early before the worst heat overtook them again.

Tallie selected a sturdy wooden spoon and returned to her worktable. "I keep telling your papa he needs to put you in a sidesaddle, but he won't listen to me. Lets you ride all over the valley like a farmhand."

"Only sissies ride sidesaddle. I have to ride spirited horses and keep them in condition. You know I have to keep Mr. Cooper's mares fit."

Tallie shook her head. "They're already fit."

"Ha! That's what you know. I haven't ridden them all week. Every one of them needs a good workout."

"Pa and me took Maude and Buttercup out yesterday," Pax said sheepishly, and Sadie stared at him.

"What? You and Zeke? You didn't tell me!"

"Mr. Oliver say they need exercise. He knows you want to ride them, but it was too hot yesterday."

Just then the dining room door opened, and her father looked in.

"Sadie, I need to see you for a moment." He turned and let the door swing to.

Sadie stared at Tallie as she fumbled with her apron strings.

"Probably nothin'." Tallie picked up her tin measuring cup and stooped over the flour bin.

"I should have gone with Papa myself." Sadie walked slowly through the dining room, across the entry, and into the parlor. A queer feeling of dread was settling in her stomach.

"Papa?"

He was sitting in his armchair, and he looked up from the paper in his hand. His solemn expression did nothing to dispel her anxiety. "Sit down, daughter."

Sadie took one of the side chairs. She wanted to ask him what was wrong, but she waited, clutching a handful of the gray fabric of her housedress. They sat in silence for a long moment, and her father stared down at the sheet of paper. She saw that it was a letter, and her fear multiplied.

"Papa?"

He looked at her then, and she could see tears standing in his eyes. "It's Tenley."

"No!" She left her chair and knelt beside him, grasping his arm and peering at the letter. "Tell me, Papa."

Her father swallowed hard and reached out to her. His hand shook, but he placed it on her head and stroked her hair. "I'm afraid he's gone. It was in the battle—"

"No, that can't be!"

"Hush, child. Listen to me. He was wounded in the battle for Mexico City. He didn't survive his wounds."

"But that was. . ." Sadie stared up at him, unable to accept his words. *Not Tenley!* First her mother, now her precious brother. It was too much to bear. Her chest tightened, and she had to struggle to breathe. "They captured the city almost a year ago, Papa!"

"Yes, in September." He sighed and held the letter out to her. "This is dated January first. It seems he lingered for several weeks in the field hospital; then it took his commanding officer awhile to write the letter. And who knows where this letter's been in the past six months? But it's here now, and so now we know."

She refused to look at the creased letter or read the fateful words. "No, Papa. We would have known. *I* would have known."

He shook his head helplessly. "We've all prayed so hard."

"I've prayed every day," Sadie agreed, tears choking her and making her voice crack. She leaned her forehead against her father's knee and sobbed.

"We'll get through this," he whispered, patting her shoulder. "Sadie, child, it's a cruel thing, but we've still got each other."

four

Harry tested the latch on the door of the tiny, one-room cabin. It was good enough to keep the door shut while he rode to Virginia and collected his brood mares from Oliver McEwan.

It was late August, and he'd planned to be on the road by now, but everything had taken longer than he'd anticipated. Thanks to several kind neighbors, his barn was now complete. That was the critical structure. All summer Harry had prepared timber, cut and stacked hay, and split firewood, then built a paddock. Last of all, he had thrown up the little cabin that would shelter him this winter. He'd planned a bigger building—a real house—but setbacks in building and haying had cut short the time he could spend on it, and he'd settled for this barely adequate cabin. No matter. He would add on to it next spring.

The important thing now was to bring the mares home. McEwan had agreed to have them bred to drop spring foals and ready to go when he arrived. In his mind's eye, Harry could see the mares trotting across his pasture with their colts at their sides. Of course, he had yet to fence the pasture, but he ought to be able to do that before cold weather set in.

He sighed and looked out over his property. There was still so much to do! He'd better not linger too long at McEwans', tempting as the thought was.

The image of Sadie in her rose-colored gown came unbidden to his thoughts as it had many times since his trip to Virginia. She was a budding rose, a girl maturing into womanhood, and he could hardly wait to see the full-blown flower.

Another picture of her flashed across his consciousness then—the wild Sadie dashing out of the woods on that exquisite mare then hauling back on the reins in a desperate effort to avoid disaster. Then the subdued Sadie, lying in the dust and looking up at him cautiously, gasping for breath while he tried not to stare.

Harry stooped to pick up his tools. He would leave at first light. He didn't want to put the trip off any longer or delay seeing her.

❧

"Papa, are you all right?"

Her father had dismounted and stood beside the stallion, pressing his fist against his lower back. He gave out a sigh and smiled at her. "Just growing old."

"It's Clipper's rough trot that's getting to you."

"You may be right." He eyed the horse critically. "He looks so good, but his gaits are downright painful."

"Not to mention that little bucking trick he does if you touch his flanks."

He gave her a rueful smile. He'd been trying to break Clipper of that habit, with no success.

Zeke came from the barn and reached for the horse's reins. "Let me walk him, Mr. Oliver. Pax, you get Miss Sadie's horse."

"Nonsense. I can cool down my own mount." Sadie clucked to Lily and led her along behind Zeke across the barnyard. She knew her father was wondering if he'd made a mistake in keeping Clipper as a stallion, but he wouldn't discuss such matters with her. Clipper was young, only four years old, and had been earmarked to replace their aging stallion, Star. In Sadie's opinion, there would never be another horse like Star, but she knew he was getting on in years, and the farm's income depended on the McEwans finding another exceptional stallion soon.

She glanced back at her father. He seemed to move a little slower since the letter had come from Tenley's commander, and Sadie was startled to note that his hair was graying quickly. Throughout the month of August, he had thrown himself into the work of the farm, and Sadie began to worry. He was working too hard. His grief drove him, she knew. Tenley's death had devastated him, but instead of languishing in his sorrow, he spent long hours in the fields and at the barn, working with the horses, haying, and most recently harvesting wheat and oats.

She had begged him to hire more help, but he had insisted he could do the work with Zeke and his two sons, Pax and Ephraim, the older son who lived a few miles away. Ephraim eked out a living for his young family as a blacksmith, but every summer he devoted a few weeks to work on the McEwan farm.

Zeke turned ahead of her and walked toward the barn with Clipper straining at the lead rope. Her father had given the stallion a good run, but he was still dancing and tossing his head. He reached over to nip Zeke's sleeve, and Zeke slapped him on the nose.

"Quit that, hoss!" Zeke glanced at Sadie. "Your papa ought to sell this one for a racehorse. That all he's good for."

"Pa!" Pax shouted.

Sadie jerked her head to stare at him. Pax was standing just inside the barn door, and he appeared to be wrestling with her father.

No, she realized in horror, Pax was holding her father up, keeping him from falling to the ground.

"Pa, help!"

"Zeke!" Sadie shrieked. Lily snorted and shied, and ahead of them Clipper neighed and reared. Zeke kept his hold on the lead rope and yanked down on it firmly.

"Ho, you hoss! Easy now."

Sadie realized she had broken one of her father's ironclad barn rules. Instead of helping in an emergency, she had screamed and caused the volatile stallion to panic.

She ran in agonizing slowness toward Pax and her father, pulling Lily along with her. "Come on, Lily! Come!" She would not break another rule and drop the lead rope. Loose horses would only cause more mayhem.

As she ran, she saw her father slide from Pax's grasp and crumple to the straw-strewn floor.

Dear God, no!

A fractured prayer left her heart as she thrust Lily's reins into Pax's hands and knelt beside her father.

❧

"Mr. Cooper's here, sugar." Tallie smiled in apology from the doorway to Sadie's bedroom.

Sadie wiped a tear away. "He's really here?"

"He just rode up to the barn. My Zeke is taking his horse. He'll show him the mares so Mr. Cooper can see how nice and fat they are; then he'll show him to the house."

Sadie nodded and pushed herself up out of the rocking chair.

"What am I going to do, Tallie?"

"Why, the same as your papa would do."

"But everything's changed now that Papa's dead."

"I know, child." Tallie opened her arms wide, and Sadie flew into them with a sob.

"What if he doesn't want to buy the mares anymore?"

"Of course he does! If he didn't, he'd have sent your papa a letter."

Sadie nodded and sniffed, and Tallie turned to open a small inlaid box on top of Sadie's dresser. She took out a clean muslin handkerchief and handed it to her.

"Here now, mop your face. You need to look your best when you greet him."

Sadie pulled in a shaky breath. "What if he wants his money back? Because—"

"Whoa now! You just borrowin' trouble. That man came for his horses, and you're gonna give them to him. He gives you the money, and that's that."

Sadie nodded and exhaled slowly. *That's that,* she thought. It wasn't at all how she had pictured her second meeting with Harry Cooper. She had imagined her father would invite him to spend the night again so they could enjoy another long evening of conversation. She'd thought she would at least have a chance to sit at dinner with him again. She'd planned it for months, down to the menu Tallie would prepare and the imported lace on her gown.

"You freshen up," Tallie said. "Put on your new blue dress. I'll go down and start the fried chicken for supper."

"No, Tallie, not the fried chicken."

Tallie stared at her. "Why not? Just like you said, Miss Sadie. Fried chicken, biscuits, butter beans, and carrots, then the pies. He liked my pie, remember?"

"I remember, but, Tallie, I can't invite him to stay to dinner tonight."

Tallie pressed her lips together. "Well, maybe not." Her shoulders drooped as she left the room.

Sadie stared into the mirror over her vanity. How could she face Harry with these red eyes and this haggard face? And yet she didn't have the energy to try to do anything about it.

❧

At last Harry got Zeke to stop extolling the virtues of the McEwan horses and take him to the house. He was a bit surprised and disappointed that Oliver hadn't come out to the barn on his arrival, but Zeke had explained that his boss had been "poorly."

"Will I be able to see Mr. McEwan?" Harry asked as they entered the house and Zeke steered him toward the parlor.

"Oh, I don't think Mr. Oliver can see you today." Zeke shook his head with doleful regret.

Sadie jumped up from a chair and stood facing Harry as he entered the room.

"Miss Sadie. How wonderful to see you again." He stepped forward eagerly and tried to hide his dismay. She wore a fetching ice blue crinoline dress, but her face was pale and drawn, and her hair was poorly dressed, put up in a loose knot from which tendrils were escaping. She must have been at her father's bedside.

"Mr. Cooper," she murmured, and Harry bent over her hand.

"I'm sorry to hear that your father is ill."

Sadie stared past him at Zeke with a look of shock. Had she expected the servant to hide the fact that his master was gravely ill?

"I—"

Her face flooded with color, and Harry smiled as a trace of the old, excitable Sadie appeared. Zeke had embarrassed her, no question, and Harry determined to do whatever he could to put her at ease.

"Do you have a few minutes?" he asked.

She hesitated then nodded. "Won't you sit down?" When she led him to a seat near the fireplace, he looked up at the painting on the front wall and smiled.

"I've thought many times of that picture this summer. I confess there were many evenings when I longed to be back here again."

Sadie swallowed. She seemed to be struggling with every word today.

"I—I hope you found the mares in good condition."

"Excellent, thank you. Miss McEwan, if your father is too ill for guests today, perhaps I can stay in town tonight and come back in the morning."

"Mr. Cooper," she said, eyeing him carefully, "I must tell you that our family has suffered a great tragedy."

He nodded, his heart filled with sympathy. "I'm so sorry about your brother. Zeke told me you received the news a few weeks ago, and it distressed me. I know how much you loved him."

Sadie bit her lip, and he thought she was holding back tears. He stood hastily. He longed to stay there and try to be a small comfort to her, but a gentleman would not presume to do that. A gentleman would express his condolences and leave.

"Miss McEwan, forgive me for intruding at this time. I'll come back tomorrow, and perhaps your father will be able to see me then."

"Oh no, really, Mr. Cooper, he won't be able to. You see—"

Zeke stepped forward. "Mr. Oliver is restin'."

Sadie stared at him. "Zeke!"

He shrank back toward the doorway, his hands folded and his eyes downcast.

Sadie cleared her throat and looked up at him, and Harry's heart pounded. She was the Sadie he remembered, even though she was grieving for her brother and worried sick about her father's health.

"You see, Mr. Cooper, Papa's heart hasn't been strong lately, and. . .and. . ."

She sobbed, and Harry couldn't help stepping closer and touching her shoulder ever so lightly.

"Don't distress yourself. I'll come back tomorrow."

She sobbed once more. "Perhaps it's best."

He nodded and backed away, not wanting to leave her, yet determined to abide by the social code. He would do nothing to upset or offend her family. At all costs, he wanted to stay in the good graces of the McEwans. Seeing Sadie again, even in her sorrow, had taught him that. If he had his way, this would not be his last visit to the Spinning Wheel Farm.

Zeke walked slightly behind him on the way to the barn.

Harry wondered if Sadie would chastise the servant later for being too forthcoming. Dark clouds were forming over the ridge of mountains in the west, and Pax was leading two horses in from the pasture. When they reached the barn he brought out Harry's horse, Pepper, and Zeke silently brought the saddle.

"I take it Mr. McEwan's condition is very grave," Harry said. He took the bridle from Zeke's hand. "Here, I can do that."

"Well, suh," Zeke said, "it ain't good. A few days back, Mr. Oliver just collapsed. Right over there." He pointed toward the barn door.

"Has he seen a doctor?"

"Ain't no doctor close, suh."

Harry frowned, wishing there was a way to help. He liked Oliver McEwan and had felt they might be friends if they lived closer. And his daughter. . .that was another story.

"Is there anything I can do, Zeke?"

"I don't think so. But if you's coming back tomorrow, I'll keep your mares in so they'll be ready for you in the mornin'."

"Thank you, Zeke. It looks like we're in for a storm tonight. I expect there's an inn in Winchester?"

"Yes, suh."

Harry nodded. "All right. I'll come back midmorning. If Mr. McEwan can't see me then. . ."

Zeke said quickly, "Miss Sadie, she can do business just like her papa. That gal can ride like the best, and she's not afraid of work. She's had it hard these last few weeks, with the bad news and all, but she's strong, Miss Sadie. She'll get through this trouble."

Harry smiled at his enthusiasm. "Yes, she's got character. I expect she'll weather the storm."

five

"What are we going to do?" Sadie asked, watching from the parlor window as Harry rode down the lane. Was she also bereft of Harry now? Her sadness weighed on her, a heavy burden pressing on her heart.

"I dunno, Miss Sadie." Tallie stood next to her, holding the lace curtain back.

"I just wish I knew what Papa would do."

"Why, he'd sell that gen'leman some hosses, of course," Zeke said from the doorway.

They both turned toward him.

"You think so?" Sadie faltered. Never in her life had she been called upon to make important decisions. Could she go forward, as her father would have, do business, and bring in money to keep the farm going?

"I know so. This gen'leman said he prayed and asked God to show him where to buy. Seems like you're the answer to his prayer, and he might be the answer to yours, too."

"What do you mean, Zeke?" Sadie felt a blush coming on. Was Zeke implying that she should pursue Harry? Was a husband the solution to her problems?

"I just mean you need cash right now, Miss Sadie. You know your papa already spent most of what he got for that colt last month. You'll need some money to get you through the winter."

She gulped. "Do you think I can stay here alone?"

"Child, you won't be alone." Tallie slipped her arm around Sadie's shoulders. "You've said before we's your family. Well, now is the time you need us. It'd be different if you had kin close by, but you don't."

Sadie nodded. "Oh, Tallie, what would I do without you and Zeke?"

"Likely you'd be just fine, Miss Sadie. But you's better with us here."

"That's so."

Zeke smiled down at her. "Don't forget your heavenly Father, Miss Sadie."

"Of course not."

"That's right," said Tallie. "You talk to Him every day, and He'll tell you what to do."

Sadie sighed. "Right now everything seems so jumbled that I don't know where to begin. And you shouldn't have lied to Mr. Cooper. You know that, Zeke."

"It wasn't a lie," Zeke said, his eyes wide in surprise.

"Listen to you!" Tallie scowled at him with evident disapproval.

"I said Mr. Oliver is restin'. Well, he is. Permanently."

Sadie felt she was helpless to change Zeke's way of looking at things. She looked to Tallie for support.

"You just should have told him straight out," Tallie said, shaking her head.

"I think it's better this way. We don't know Mr. Cooper very well."

Tallie arched her back and glared at him. "That man is a gen'leman, and you know it!"

"Well, I do like Mr. Harry." Zeke scratched his chin. "I don't expect Miss Sadie needs protectin' from him."

"I should say not!" Tallie was not mollified, Sadie could tell. The woman had appointed herself Harry's champion, and besides that, she was obviously disappointed he hadn't stayed to dinner.

"When he comes back tomorrow, I'll tell him the truth," Sadie said. "If he doesn't want to do business with me, I can't help it, but I won't continue this lie, Zeke."

Zeke had the grace to look down at the floor. "I'm sorry, Miss Sadie. I didn't mean to deceive. I did tell Mr. Harry you'll be speakin' to your Father tonight about his business deal, though."

"You *what*? Zeke, how could you do that?"

"Easy now, missy." Zeke held out his hands beseechingly. "I just thought you'd be talkin' to your heavenly Father. You know you're on good speakin' terms with Him."

"Well, of course. But—"

"So I put Mr. Harry at ease. He was askin' for particulars on Mr. Oliver, and I cogitated he'd feel better about the whole thing if I told him that." He looked up at Sadie and said quickly, "And it weren't no lie. You will be asking the Almighty what to do, won't you, Miss Sadie?"

"Well, of course." She looked uncomfortably at Tallie.

"The truth, Zeke," Tallie said. "The truth is always the best. You know that."

Zeke shrugged, and his wife sighed in exasperation.

"Fine," Zeke said. "I just thought that poor Miss Sadie didn't need to be tellin' menfolk who aren't much more than strangers that she's got nobody here to protect her now. And we don't know what will happen to Mr. Oliver's property, with Mr. Tenley gone and all. It just seemed to me that until she finds out what will become of the estate—"

Tallie's dark eyes threw defiant sparks at him. "We can take care of Miss Sadie! Whatever happens to her, she has us and the good Lawd!"

❧

After a mediocre dinner at the inn, Harry settled into a tiny attic room under the eaves. He'd chosen this accommodation over sharing a larger, more comfortable room on the second floor with a team of surveyors.

A deafening bolt of thunder cracked as Harry reached his room. He blew out the candle the landlady had given him and stared out the window. He was glad he'd found the livery stable and seen to Pepper's care early. His horse shouldn't be too uneasy, although the high winds worried Harry a bit. A few scattered papers blew about the street below, and as he watched, a limb was torn from a large elm tree across the way. It was early for the trees to shed their foliage, but the wind whipped the leaves so hard that many loosed their hold and flew with the maelstrom.

A scattered pattering of rain on the roof above him became a roar as the clouds dumped their load and millions of drops pounded down on the shingles. His room had no ceiling, just the underside of the boards of the roof, and Harry eyed them speculatively, wondering if the shingles on top would hold their places. The rain pummeled the street, turning the powdery dust to muddy soup in minutes, and a change in the wind sent a torrent of water against his window, sheeting down the glass before him.

Harry sighed and stretched out on the rickety cot. He wondered how the folks at McEwans' were doing. He ought to have stayed there. With Oliver so ill, Zeke and Pax would need help with the chores and making certain everything at the farm was battened down before the storm.

Sadie would be right out there with them, helping secure the livestock, he was sure, and Tallie would be in the kitchen. No matter what the weather, Tallie would conjure up a huge, tasty meal, one much better than the poor fare he'd found at the inn. Miserable excuses for biscuits they had here, and the stew was composed of overcooked vegetables and some unidentifiable meat. It was worse than what had come out of the galley of the *Swallow*. The more he thought about it, the more certain he was that Pax, the half-grown servant boy at McEwans', had eaten much better than he had this night. Yes, and he probably had a cozier berth, too.

Harry was too restless to sleep, and the intermittent thunder and surges of rain would have kept him awake anyway. He got up and stood at the window again. Great. Pepper would probably have to slog through five miles of mud in the morning. But he knew it was more than Tallie's cooking and more even than the four superior mares he was buying that drew him to the Spinning Wheel Farm.

Sadie, his heart cried out. *Lord, I don't know what it is about that gal, but I truly believe You engineered our first meeting. Something inside me is mourning with her. I want to see her carefree and eager for life again.*

His anticipation had grown all summer and had peaked as he approached the farm that afternoon. But his eagerness had dissipated when he saw her again, and his brief meeting with Sadie had been a disappointment. Something was wrong there, very wrong.

Of course her father was sick, perhaps fatally so, and it was only a few weeks since she'd learned of her brother's death. Still, he couldn't forget the wariness and melancholy in Sadie's eyes today. She was not the cheerful, outgoing girl he'd remembered and dreamed of all summer. In fact she'd seemed almost frightened of him today. She hadn't been that way in May. Had he imagined the spark in her eyes back then and the secret smiles they had shared over a simple game of dominoes? No, it was real. She had regretted the parting as much as he had.

He lay down again, determined to catch some sleep. As soon as it was daylight he would go for Pepper and head back to the farm. If she still held him off, he would pay for the mares and leave. But he hoped. . . .

Harry sighed. What did he hope exactly? That Oliver would be well enough to see him, of course, and that their business would be concluded satisfactorily. But that was secondary, he knew, to his longing to see Sadie's eyes light up. He had hoped to deepen his acquaintance with her—there was no denying it. If he were honest, he would admit he had hoped he would find her receptive to his interest. A courtship even? It would have to be either a short one or a protracted one conducted long distance.

But he knew he had at least hoped for encouragement, and he hadn't gotten that today. He closed his eyes. There was only one place to turn when things weren't going the way he planned. After all, God was in charge of these events, from the long-decided battle in Mexico to the storm that tore at the inn and made the timbers shudder.

❧

Sadie sat up in bed, shivering. She fumbled in the darkness to light her bedside candle. The thunder didn't frighten her exactly, but she didn't like being alone in the big house during the violent storm. She felt isolated and vulnerable.

Tallie and Zeke were battened down in their little house beyond the big barn. The house had been two slave cabins in the old days. Zeke and her father had torn them apart and made one snug little dwelling from the lumber years ago, before Sadie was born. Zeke and Tallie had raised their five children there, and Sadie had played with them all. The girls had kept watch of her while her mother was busy. Pax, the youngest, was the only one left in their home now, and Sadie knew he was warm and dry in his loft above his parents' small bedroom.

A sharp crack made her jump, and she heard lightning strike nearby. She threw back the covers and hurried to the window, gazing out over the yard. She couldn't see anything amiss, but she wished Tallie had stayed in the big house with her tonight.

As she stared out into the darkness, she made out rivulets of water coursing across the barnyard and down the lane. The trees near the pasture fence tossed fitfully. The booming of closer lightning strikes now and then drowned out the rumbling background of thunder.

She reached for the woolen coverlet her grandmother had woven and pulled it around her. It was chilly, but she knew that if she stayed in bed she would only toss and turn.

She thought back to the event that had consumed her mind today. Harry Cooper was in town. He would be back in the morning. Tears filled her eyes as she realized how the long-awaited day had turned to ashes. She would have only one brief chance to set things straight with him. She wanted to, but she wasn't sure how he would receive her news.

And when he had gone, what would become of her then? She had to think beyond Harry's visit, to tomorrow and the next day and the rest of her life. Would she be forced to leave here soon? Did she even have a right to be here now? Would she have to seek a new place to live and a way to support herself that did not include the farm?

Dear Lord, she prayed silently, *there's so much I need Your help with. Please give me wisdom and show me what to do.*

She felt calmer and a bit more optimistic. She sat watching the flickering lightning and began to pray for those she loved, although that circle had grown quite small.

Thank You, Lord, for Tallie and Zeke. Thank You for—

Crack! Her eyes flew open, and she jumped from her chair. The sharp lightning strike was followed by a ripping, tearing crash that rocked the house.

six

Harry reined in Pepper and stared at the McEwans' house. A huge tree had apparently been torn from the towering oak tree on the south side of the house and was now wedged in the upper story. The roof had been torn open, exposing the interior of one of the bedchambers. Unless he was mistaken, it was Tenley's room where he had spent a comfortable night last spring.

Harry spurred his gelding into a gallop and tore up the lane, searching all the while for movement amidst the rubble. There was Zeke, climbing over the debris. Relief swept over Harry, and he halted Pepper once more.

"Zeke! Hey, Zeke!"

The black man straightened and peered down at him from between the branches of the oak. His face opened in a wide grin, and he waved with enthusiasm.

"Mr. Cooper! Hello, suh!"

"Anyone hurt?" Harry called.

"No, suh. The good Lawd was choosy about where He dropped this limb."

Harry smiled and dismounted. "I'll put Pepper in the barn and come help you."

"No need, suh. I'll send my boy to tend him." Harry saw then that Pax was also in the shambles with his father, pulling at the wreckage.

"No, I'll do it myself; then I'm coming up there to help you."

Zeke grinned down at him. "As you say, Mr. Harry. Just make yourself to home, suh. We'll tell Miss Sadie you're here, and she can see you in the dinin' room when you come in. The parlor window's broke, but that's all right. Won't take much to fix that."

Harry relaxed then, knowing Zeke had accepted his presence. He led Pepper toward the large barn, stepping around the biggest puddles.

"All right, fella," he said, opening the half door to the first empty stall he came to. "I know you're muddy and tired, but you'll be all right in here for a while." He noted with satisfaction that the manger was filled with hay. "I'll bring you some water in a while and clean you up."

Pepper whinnied and poked his head out over the Dutch door, snorting when another horse stuck his head out of a stall farther down the aisle.

Sadie met him at the door to the house.

"Mr. Cooper, it's good of you to offer to help us, but Zeke can—"

Harry brushed her protest aside and stepped into the entry. "Nonsense, Miss McEwan. Your roof is severely damaged. It will take days to clear out the mess and make it weather-tight again."

Sadie hesitated, and he smiled down at her.

"Please let me help. I'm here, and I'm strong. There's no way I'm leaving without lending a hand. Let me do what I can today."

She bit her bottom lip and nodded. "All right. Thank you. I admit, it's too big a job for us."

He saw she was wearing a patched apron over a worn gray dress. The hemline and sleeves were a bit shorter than was customary, and he guessed she had put on an old, outgrown dress so she could join in the work. A suggestion of plaster dust tinged her rich hair where it peeped out from beneath a cotton scarf. Harry looked into her blue eyes and felt the same spark of joy he'd known in May when he'd first seen her. She was the same Sadie, after all, even with all the trials she had encountered.

Her long lashes swept down over her eyes, and she stepped aside with a sudden air of shyness. "Let me show you upstairs. Zeke can tell you best what needs to be done. There's a lot of water damage. Tallie and I have been getting out the bedclothes and rugs to try to salvage them."

He followed her up the stairway, questions flooding his mind. "Was your father's bedroom damaged?"

"No." She stepped up into the second floor hallway and turned partway toward him. "Mr. Cooper, Father is—" She looked at him then away.

"He's not injured then?"

"No, but—"

She turned away, bringing one hand quickly to her lips, and Harry wished he hadn't spoken. Apparently Oliver was no better today.

"I'm sorry, Sadie," he said softly.

She gave him a watery smile and seemed about to speak again when Zeke clumped out of the wrecked room in his rough boots.

"Mr. Harry, I have to say I'm glad to see you, suh!"

He smiled and extended his hand. "I'll be glad to help any way I can."

Zeke hesitated, looking at him with a question, and then clasped his hand. "I thank you, suh."

"Since Mr. Cooper insists, I suppose we'd be foolish to turn down his offer of help." Sadie pushed aside an oak branch and wriggled into the room. "Zeke, I think we can dismantle the bedstead and take the pieces out of here."

"We'll do that, Miss Sadie, soon's we cut a few more limbs away. Whyn't you and Tallie see if you can find a sheet of canvas to hang over that parlor window. I misdoubt we'll be able to go for glass today. Too much to clear away up here."

He nodded sagely at Harry. "Good thing you spent the night in town, suh."

"Truly spoken." Harry looked at the bed in grateful awe. The heavy oak branch must be a third part of the ancient tree. It had smashed through the roof and front wall of the room diagonally, crushing the armoire that had stood near the window and cracking at least one of the bed rails. The heaviest part lay across Tenley's bed, and a gnarled limb gouged deep into the mattress where Harry's chest would have been if he had slept there.

Zeke placed a saw in his hand, and he set about cutting the smaller branches off the huge fallen limb. He put Sadie out of his thoughts and concentrated on the job. Zeke sent Pax down to the lawn in front of the porch to gather up the wood they threw down and stack it around behind the house near the kitchen door.

The tear in the roof extended over the bedroom and a storage room, but the ridge pole seemed solid, and Harry agreed with Zeke that only the east half of the roof's front side would need replacing. The outer walls of the bedroom would need new framing timbers, and the plaster would have to be redone, as well. The sashes and glass in two upstairs windows were destroyed, in addition to the parlor window below, and the whitewash would need to be freshened when the repairs were completed.

"I can work on the inside this winter if need be," Zeke said after an hour's work. "If we can get the roof fixed before another storm, we'll be in good shape."

Harry stooped to examine the frame of the bed. "I think we can get this out of here now. You'll have to mend this side rail, but the damage isn't too bad, considering."

Zeke went to the doorway and called, "Miss Sadie! Miss Sadie, where you say you want this here bedstead?"

Harry wrestled the plump featherbed off onto the floor. By

the time he had the footboard separated from the side rails, she was in the room.

She directed Zeke on where to take the featherbed then turned to Harry. "Just follow me, Mr. Cooper."

Harry picked up the heavy footboard and carried it carefully through the doorway and to the opposite end of the hallway. She opened a pristine white door and stepped into another bedchamber.

He knew at once that it was her room. Even without her sidelong glance and the becoming pink of her cheeks, he'd have known. The embroidered bed hangings were embellished with decidedly feminine lilac blossoms, and a green gown was hanging on the door of the armoire. He made himself quit looking around as his curiosity seemed to raise her anxiety.

"Just lean it against the wall there." She nodded toward the longest stretch of bare wall.

Harry set the footboard down and straightened. He couldn't help noticing an old spinning wheel in one corner. "That's a very old piece, isn't it?" he asked, more to relieve her uneasiness than anything else. "Do you spin?"

"No. It belonged to my great-grandmother Walsh. My grandmother used to spin wool on it, and my mother did some when she was a girl. I never learned, but I asked Papa if I could keep it."

He nodded and stepped over to give the wheel a spin. "It's in good condition. My mother used to spin, too."

They smiled at each other, a small, tentative smile on Sadie's part, but it sent his pulse racing. Given enough time, he was sure he could regain the ground he'd lost with her since May. But time was the one thing he wouldn't have with Sadie.

She ran her hand over the scarf that covered her hair. "I'd best go help Tallie."

"I'll bring the rest of the bed in here."

He met Zeke in the hallway, awkwardly carrying the

headboard. Harry grabbed one end and walked backward along to Sadie's room. When they had set it down with the footboard, they made their way back to the scene of destruction.

"I can get the rails and slats," Zeke said.

Harry nodded, surveying the room. They had sawn up the lesser limbs and thrown the wood down into the yard below. Just the main part of the big oak limb was left, and it would take a lot of energy to cut it in pieces small enough to toss out.

The cherry armoire had been smashed by the falling tree, and a small side table and lamp were broken. The washstand seemed to be unscathed except for some scratches on the wood. The porcelain bowl and pitcher stood miraculously unharmed in the corner of the room farthest from the breach.

"This was a beautiful room," Harry said, shaking his head.

"Yes, suh." Zeke wiped the sweat from his forehead with his sleeve then glanced up through the gaping roof toward the sun. "I'd best get down to the barn. Those animals had ought to be put out to pasture now that the weather's cleared."

"Would you like me to help you, or should I stay here and keep on with this?" Harry asked.

Zeke looked around. "It's gonna be a big job, ain't it, Mr. Harry? I don't think we can fix this roof today."

"No, we can't. But I can measure what we'll need for timbers while you're at the barn. Do you have a measuring line, Zeke?"

"Mr. Oliver has one. I'll ask Tallie to see if she can find it. We'll have to get some lumber and shingles." Zeke headed for the stairs.

"I'd better go and see to my own horse," Harry said.

"My boy and I can tend him, if you want."

Harry hesitated. "If you don't mind."

"Not a bit, Mr. Harry."

"All right, thank you. Could you see that he gets a drink of water then?"

"Yes, suh, I'll do that. If you want, I'll have Pax put him out to grass after."

When Zeke returned, Harry had made a careful inspection of the damage and prepared a list of the lumber he estimated they would need to complete the restoration. Zeke sent Pax to the sawmill two miles downriver with a wagon and Harry's list. The two men tackled the heavy log that was the last of the tree limb. When it had been sawn into manageable pieces and ousted, they began clearing away the ragged, broken boards and plaster in preparation for the repairs. By noon Harry was certain he and Zeke had become lifelong friends. They worked well together, with few words needed between them.

Sadie appeared in the doorway. "I've got a basin of water at the back door so you gentlemen can wash up for dinner."

"I don't know," Harry said with a grin. "It might take the whole Shenandoah River to get us clean."

Zeke laughed and brushed at the plaster on his sleeve, but it was damp and mushy from his exposure to the rain-soaked room.

"Yep, we are two filthy field hands. I expect we'd both best eat in the kitchen, Miss Sadie."

"We're all eating in the kitchen, although Tallie's a mite scandalized." Sadie shot a sideways glance at Harry. "No offense, sir, but the time it would take us all to clean up and change—"

"I agree," Harry said. "Especially when we'll be coming back to this job as soon as we're finished eating."

He bowed solemnly and gestured toward the hallway. "After you, sir."

Zeke grinned. "No, suh, you first."

Sadie was not in evidence when they passed through the

kitchen. Tallie looked at Zeke, her eyebrows arched high. "You done gone and turned Mr. Harry into a no-account."

Zeke laughed. "He's a hardworking no-account."

When they reached the lean-to at the back door, Harry peeled off his shirt and shook it outside, but it was a sorry mess. If he was still there for the evening meal, he'd have to retrieve his extra clothing from his pack in the barn. He splashed water from the tin basin over his face and hands.

"I hope Mr. McEwan wasn't disturbed by all the racket we've been making this morning." He reached for one of the towels Sadie had left on the bench beside the basin.

Zeke tossed the water onto the row of zinnias outside the lean-to and refilled the basin for himself from a bucket. "Oh, no, suh, I can assure you, Mr. Oliver wasn't disturbed by us."

"Glad to hear it. I asked Miss Sadie about her father, but she seems quite distressed about his condition. I don't like to press her."

"Well, I can tell you, Mr. Oliver is no different today than he was the last few days, and the storm and all didn't bother him a bit."

Harry nodded, thinking about that. It seemed to him that a man would have to be comatose not to have been disturbed by the jolt the house had taken in the night.

His muscles ached from the morning's labor, but sinking into the sturdy oak chair across from Sadie for lunch was worth every minute of work. She had washed her face, brushed her hair to a luster, and removed the faded apron. It was hard to decide which reward was better—Tallie's cooking or Sadie's shy smile.

❧

They were all exhausted by suppertime. Sadie had scrubbed and swept and mopped most of the day. When Pax returned with the lumber and nails in the middle of the afternoon, the men unloaded it all. The boy ate a late luncheon then set about splitting and stacking the rest of the wood from the oak tree. Harry and Zeke made a temporary covering over the yawning hole in the roof in case more rain came in the night. Tallie did her usual kitchen chores and helped Sadie wash the curtains, blankets, and sheets from Tenley's bedroom.

"We ought to ask Mr. Cooper to stay." As they folded the dry linens in the bright sunshine, Sadie looked to Tallie for guidance, uncertain as to what course she should take.

"Yes, you should. That man's worked like an ox all day, for nothin'."

"Can we feed him again tonight?" Sadie felt the least bit timid to ask the favor, and Tallie looked over at her as if she were crazy.

"Why, child, I've got fresh johnnycake in the oven, and I kept over the chicken and sweets I was planning to serve Mr. Harry last night. You know I forbade Zeke and Pax to touch those pies. Why you think I didn't serve them this noon?"

"I was wondering," Sadie admitted. *Those are for Mr. Cooper,* Tallie had told them last night, even though at the time Sadie was sure Harry would return briefly for his horses and be gone before another meal was served at the McEwan house. Yet Tallie had served gingerbread after luncheon this noon.

"They're for his dinner."

Sadie frowned as she pulled a linen towel from the clothesline. "Well, I can't have him stay here in the house tonight. I mean, not if I'm alone here. And he thinks—oh, Tallie, what am I going to do? Zeke has muddled everything!"

"Should have told him straight out," Tallie agreed with a shake of her head.

"I know it, but it's too late now! How would it look? Mr. Cooper would be shocked, and who knows what he'd do? He might tell someone who could do us harm, Tallie!"

"Mr. Harry wouldn't do that."

"No, I suppose not." Sadie stood in indecision. "But Tenley's room is ruined, and Papa's room is full of the extra furniture. Where would we put him, even if you slept up here for appearances?" Suddenly the tears that had hounded her for days gushed from her eyes, and Sadie sat down with a plunk on the grass and buried her face in her apron. "Tallie, I had to have Harry put the bedstead in my own room, because if he went into Papa's room. . ." She sobbed, unable to continue.

"There, child." Tallie came close and hugged her. "You've had a lot to deal with lately. There now."

"Tallie, tell me what to do!" Sadie sobbed and put her arms around Tallie. "Please tell me. I'm so tired and confused."

"Well, we's all tired, that's for sure. We can't send Mr. Harry back to town."

"No, no, we can't. Oh, Tallie, you don't think he'll ask for his money back?"

"Of course not."

"I do hope you're right, because what with having to buy lumber and all, we're going to need cash really soon."

"Your papa had nothin' at all in the bank?"

"I don't think so, and even if there's a little bit, it's not rightfully mine."

The door to the lean-to opened, and Zeke strolled out with a bucket in each hand.

"You frying that chicken tonight, sugarplum?" he asked Tallie as he headed for the well.

"Iffen I don't, it'll spoil," she replied. "I kept it in the spring house all day, but it's going in the pan shortly."

"Sounds good to me. Mr. Harry and me'll be ready to tuck into it whenever you say."

Tallie frowned at him. "Mr. Harry is eatin' in the dinin' room tonight with Miss Sadie."

"Yes, ma'am, I hear you." Zeke ambled on toward the well, but Tallie's next statement brought him to a halt.

"You quit feedin' Mr. Harry full of lies. You tryin' to wreck

Miss Sadie's prospects with that gen'leman?"

Zeke turned to face her. "I ain't told no lies."

"Oh, listen to you! Surely, surely, my ears ain't workin' right!" Tallie looked pointedly at Sadie. "You hear him say he don't lie?"

"Well, Tallie, I'm not sure Zeke intended to be deceptive, but Mr. Cooper made certain assumptions, and—"

"That's right," Zeke said. "He assumpted. Now what was I supposed to tell him, with Miss Sadie here worried sick over what's to become of her? Mr. Harry, he's a good sort, but we didn't know that for sure yesterday. Now we know it."

Tallie nodded. "A man works that hard all day for you—he's a true friend."

"That's right. He's upstairs right now workin' on that mess. And tomorrow me and Mr. Harry is going to get that roof closed in."

"Tomorrow?" Sadie blinked at Zeke. "He's coming back tomorrow?"

"Comin' back?" Zeke set his buckets down and slapped his thigh. "Miss Sadie, you not going to make that fine young man ride all the way to Winchester tonight when he's bone tired!"

"Well. . ." Sadie looked once more at Tallie and saw that Tallie was coming to a decision.

"We was just talkin' about that," Tallie said. "We got no place for Mr. Harry here in the big house."

"Well, then, he'll just have to bunk with me and Pax in our cabin, and you can join Miss Sadie for tonight," Zeke said.

"Would you?" Sadie asked, searching Tallie's face for an indication of her feelings.

Tallie's teeth gleamed as she smiled. "Why, surely! That's the answer. That is, if Mr. Harry don't care about sleepin' with the poor folks."

"Mr. Harry don't stand on ceremony," Zeke said.

"But still. . ." Sadie looked doubtfully from one to the other. She was certain it wasn't socially correct to ask a guest to sleep in the hired help's home especially when they were a black family. Mrs. Thurber would be shocked. "I—I'm just not sure. . . ." She stood up. "Oh, Tallie, I'm so tired. I don't know what's right and what's not! I suppose Zeke can ask Mr. Cooper if he's willing, and if he's insulted he can take his mares and leave."

"No worry about that," Zeke said, smiling and reaching into the pocket of his trousers. "Mr. Harry done told me he's stayin' 'til the roof is tight, and he asked me to give you this."

"What is it?"

"It's the rest of the money for the horses. He said he'd like to give it to your pa direct, but since we had these unexpected expenses and all, he thought maybe he'd best give it to you, and you can give it to your papa."

Sadie gulped and reached for the money. "I feel like I'm taking this under false pretenses."

"Nonsense, child," said Tallie. She glared at Zeke. "Mr. Harry is a fine man. He would have understood. Why did you have to muddle things up so? You ought to be sleepin' in the barn for three nights—you're so bad! If I wasn't sleepin' with Miss Sadie tonight, I surely wouldn't sleep with you! I'd makc you—"

Sadie burst into tears, and Tallie caught her breath and drew her close in her embrace. "See what you done, Zeke? Now git your water, and git on out of here. Miss Sadie's gone all weepy 'cause of you, and I've got chicken to fry!"

seven

Four days later Harry and Zeke worked side by side, nailing shingles into place on the roof. Pax went up and down the ladder, bringing them supplies. Harry's knees ached from kneeling on the staging, but he didn't dare stop hammering.

"I'm thinkin' we're in for rain before nightfall," Zeke said, casting a worried glance toward the sky.

Harry had several nails protruding from his mouth, but he grunted in reply.

"Think we can finish before it hits, Mr. Harry?"

He took the nails out and shook his head. "I doubt it. But we should be able to cover what's left with that canvas so it won't leak in."

Zeke nodded. "That's my thinkin', too."

They worked on steadily, course after course of cedar shingles.

"Got to move the staging," Zeke said at last.

Harry looked out over the valley. Dark clouds were brewing. "Maybe we'd best cover it up and get off this ridgepole before the lightning commences to look for a target."

"You think so, suh?"

In answer to Zeke's question, thunder rumbled ominously.

"Come on!" Harry stood up, flexing his back wearily. The canvas was folded back each morning and weighted down on the upper part of the roof. He and Zeke scrambled up the slant.

"Yes, suh, we'd best start makin' things shipshape," Zeke said.

Quitting early was a blessing, Harry thought. For once he'd

have time to bathe at leisure then spend a pleasant evening with Sadie. All week they'd worked until the sun set, and every night when they quit at last for supper, they were so tired they all retired as soon as the meal was finished. There was never time for a detailed conversation.

As the first raindrops pattered on the canvas, they were scooting down the ladder with their tools. They dashed inside just as Pax came sprinting up from the barn.

"Hosses all under cover," Pax told his father, and Zeke clapped him on the shoulder.

"Good boy! We'd best go wash up, or your mama won't give us any supper."

Harry was pleased to find that Tallie had carried warm water to Tenley's room for him. The chamber was still bare of furniture, and the walls needed plastering and painting, but it would do fine as a bathroom.

"I washed all your extra clothes this morning, Mr. Harry," she told him with a satisfied grin. "They dried out just in time. I brung your things in before the rain started."

"Thank you, Tallie." He hated to cause her extra work, but his two changes of clothing had become offensive from grime and sweat.

As he mounted the stairs, Sadie approached.

"Harry, since you've been so kind and stayed on to help us, I wanted to offer you these."

She held out a bundle of clothes, and he took it with mixed emotions. He badly needed the extra clothing, and he didn't want to embarrass her with his meager wardrobe. On the other hand, it must be stressful to her to offer him things that had perhaps belonged to her deceased brother.

"Sadie, I. . .this is very thoughtful of you."

She shook her head and raised one hand. "Father. . ."

"Your father suggested you give me some of Tenley's clothes?"

"No, actually. . ." She winced then took a deep breath. "These were my father's things. You're larger than Tenley. I'm afraid the cuffs of his trousers would be above your boot tops, and I don't like to contemplate your trying to fit one of his shirts."

Harry chuckled. "Well, please express my warmest thanks to your father. How is he?"

"He's. . .the same."

Harry nodded. He'd tried not to ask too often. Sadie, Zeke, and Tallie all seemed on edge when he inquired about the master of the house.

"Well," he said, and she looked up at him. Her blue eyes were trusting now, and Harry felt a sweet longing. A longing for a permanent home, not the little hut he had erected in Kentucky. A longing for many evenings with Sadie, a lifetime of cozy, companionable evenings.

"How is the roof coming?" she asked.

"Good. I think we can finish it tomorrow if it dries out enough."

"Yes. I wouldn't want you and Zeke up there if it's still wet. We don't need any accidents now."

He nodded. "If it rains, we can work inside, on the walls that need redoing. And if it's dry, we'll finish off the roof and get at those windows next."

"Harry. . ."

"Yes?"

"You don't have to stay, you know." She flushed, and he could almost read her mind. She didn't want to sound ungrateful, and she didn't truly want him to leave, but she didn't want to hold him either, if he wished to go.

"I want to stay a little longer, Sadie, and make sure you're comfortable again before I leave you."

The corners of her lips curved in a delicious smile. "Thank you," she whispered and headed down the stairs.

"Sadie!" When she turned back, he couldn't resist asking, "Are you ever going to wear that green velvet gown?"

Her face went scarlet, and he wondered if he'd been too bold in mentioning the dress he'd seen hanging in her room. He'd thought of it several times, wishing she would wear it to dinner some evening, but she hadn't. It was probably a ball gown, made for fancy parties she would attend this fall if her father's health improved. She wouldn't put the lovely creation on for a simple family dinner, but he still wanted to see her in it.

"Perhaps I shall, if you wish it, Harry."

Their gazes met, and he felt a flutter in his heart. Sadie wasn't a flirt by any means, but she was daring to respond to his suggestion.

❧

After helping Tallie set the table, Sadie went back up to her bedroom. Maybe she was taking a risk, offering Harry some of her father's clothing. Tallie had insisted he let her wash and mend his extra things that day since his clothes were filthy and his shirts were torn. She didn't want to further embarrass him by giving him the clothes, but it was silly for him to go around threadbare because he had extended his stay, when there were plenty of clothes in the house.

Be careful, Sadie, she warned herself. She liked Harry. She liked him a lot. But she mustn't lose her wariness. Harry meant her no harm, she was sure; but if he learned her secret, he might feel it was his duty to take action.

She sighed and studied her face once again in the mirror. Why did they have to deceive him? Why? But she couldn't correct things now. It had been too long. They had to go on as they were. In a sense, it would be a relief when he was gone. She wouldn't have to go on pretending anymore.

No! her heart cried. *Life will be unbearable when he's gone.*

She turned and opened her armoire. The deep green velvet

was softer than lamb's wool. Why shouldn't she wear the dress for Harry? She had planned it this way. She had sewn every stitch dreaming of the night he would see her in it. Hour after hour she had labored over the detail on the bodice, the layers of whisper-soft fabric, stitching and nurturing her dreams of Harry.

She undid the buttons of her blue dress and pulled it off. A quiet dinner tonight with Harry. Joy shot through her, and she stood still for a second then tiptoed across to the mirror again. How could she feel such anticipation and eagerness again? Was it right to feel this way? Perhaps the green velvet should wait. Tears welled up in her eyes.

Papa, I don't know how to behave anymore. I'm sorry. I want you to be proud of me.

She sat down on the edge of her bed, inhaling long, deliberate breaths. *Heavenly Father,* she prayed, *please help me to do what is right.*

A quiet tap came at the door, and she jumped up with a gasp. Here she was, lolling about in her underclothes.

"Miss Sadie," Tallie called.

"Yes?"

"Mr. Kauffman is in the parlor, inquirin' after you and Mr. Oliver."

Sadie swallowed hard. "I'm dressing, Tallie."

"I'll tell him you be right down. He don't expect to stay long. He's just on his way home from town and stopped in."

Sadie quickly put the blue dress on again. She would feel foolish going down to meet her stolid neighbor wearing the lavish gown. And besides, later on, after things had calmed down a bit, he might recall seeing her in a fancy evening dress this night. *No,* she decided, *it's not proper. Thank You, Lord, for sending Mr. Kauffman.*

As she entered the parlor a few minutes later, Zeke was placing a cup of tea in her neighbor's hands. Mr. Kauffman's clothes and hair were damp, and she realized he'd turned in at the lane as much for shelter from the rain as for a neighborly visit. Perhaps she ought to invite him to stay to dinner. Her heart sank at the thought of losing that intimate hour at the table with Harry.

"No, suh," Zeke said, "Mr. Oliver's no better today, but he's no worse."

The farmer caught sight of Sadie and rose. "My dear, I'm sorry we've neglected you so. I had no idea you received such severe damage in the storm last week. Zeke was just telling me about all you've been going through, and your father so ill."

"It's all right," she faltered. "We've been managing."

"But you could have used some help!"

"That's all right, suh," Zeke said, "We've had a guest helping us."

"A guest?" Mr. Kauffman looked at Zeke then at Sadie.

"Well, yes." Sadie could feel the heat flooding her face at the mention of Harry, but she supposed Zeke was right; there was no point in concealing Harry's visit. It would only look bad later if people found out he had been here for nearly a week, and she hadn't mentioned it to anyone. "Mr. Cooper was here to see Papa on business when we had the storm damage, and he's been helping Zeke with the carpentry work."

Zeke nodded, smiling at her. "That's right. And Miss Sadie's Father says—"

"Zeke!" Sadie glared at him. She would not stand by and listen to him add to the lie they were living.

"But, Miss Sadie," he said in an injured tone, "you know you been speakin' to your Father about all this business, and He been tellin' you things will be all right. Isn't that what you told me this mornin'?" His meaningful stare pierced her heart.

Sadie swallowed hard. She had mentioned to Tallie and Zeke that her prayers had been a great comfort to her and that God had assured her of His care for her and her people.

"Well, I—" She heard a light step behind her and turned. Harry was entering the parlor with an inquisitive air.

Suddenly Sadie knew she couldn't bear it any longer. She could not, *would not*, stand there and imply things that were not true. And yet she couldn't blurt out the truth in front of Mr. Kauffman. She felt as though she couldn't breathe.

"Excuse me!" She pushed past Harry and dashed through the doorway, across the hall, and out the front door. She ran through the yard, aware that the rain had slackened to a light mist.

She pushed open the barn door and ducked inside. It was dark and warm inside, with the homey sounds of horses chewing their evening rations and the smells of manure, leather, and sweet hay. How many times had she found solace in the company of horses?

Harry's gelding, Pepper, was in the stall nearest the door on the right, and she stepped toward him. His large head was a dark bulk in the dimness, and he nickered softly. Sadie reached up and stroked his long, soft nose. Little sobs began low in her chest and made their way up her throat, escaping in gasps. She leaned her arms on the half door of the stall and wept, not caring that Pepper was snuffling at her hair.

Everything was wrong, and she couldn't fix any of it.

"Sadie."

She caught her breath and raised her head.

"Sadie?"

Harry was standing very close to her, and she sniffed. The one moment in the last four months when she didn't want Harry within a mile of her, and he'd found her.

eight

"Come here." Harry's warm fingers closed on Sadie's wrist, and she did not resist his gentle pull but went into his strong arms and let him hold her while she sobbed. He stroked her hair and her shoulders, saying nothing. Sadie found her anguish subsiding as she absorbed the warm, solid security of Harry's embrace.

At last she straightened and pulled back a few inches, but he kept his firm hold on her. She fumbled in her pocket for a handkerchief and chased her tears with it.

"I'm sorry, Harry. I've soaked your clean shirt."

"It's all right." He pulled her back in against his chest, and she went willingly.

"Is Mr. Kauffman all in a dither?"

"No, but he's heading home. The rain's let up, and he expressed his condolences."

"What did you tell him? About me, I mean? I shouldn't have left you to make my excuses." Perhaps she should have asked what Zeke said to Mr. Kauffman, she thought bitterly. Wasn't this all Zeke's fault?

"I just told him things have been difficult for you. I think he understood."

"Thank you."

"He offered to send his two sons over to help with the roofing—"

"Oh, dear! They're not coming, are they?"

He smiled. "No, I assured him we were doing fine, and he admitted he needs his boys on the harvest right now."

Sadie sighed in relief. Wilfred Kauffman ogled her every

time he had a chance, and it was very disconcerting. She realized suddenly that she was clinging to Harry, her arms encircling his waist, and she jerked away from him, appalled at her behavior. "Harry, I—"

He bent toward her, and Sadie caught her breath. He was going to kiss her. It caught her off guard, but in a flash she knew she had longed for this second. For one instant, all thoughts of propriety fled. There was only Harry for that moment, that one long, delightful moment when anything seemed possible, even a carefree future.

Her wickedness struck her suddenly, and she tore away from him with a gasp. It was terribly wrong for her to let him assume things could be good and sweet between them when she had been lying to him for more than a week now.

❧

Harry let her leave his arms with a pang of regret. It was too soon—that much was clear.

"I'm sorry, Sadie. Please forgive me."

She stood before him in silence. He could barely see her face in the dimness of the barn, but he could feel the confusion in her hesitation, and he could hear her breath coming in shallow gulps.

"I'm. . .not angry with you," she said.

He reached out and brushed her cheek with the backs of his fingers. "I should have spoken to your father first, but you know that's been impossible. It just. . .it seemed like the right moment, but I know how distressed you've been. This isn't the right time, after all, is it?"

She sobbed once more and raised the handkerchief quickly to her lips, as though to smother the sound. "Please, Harry. I don't think I can go on like this. Maybe it's time for you to leave."

He stood still, trying to take it in. She didn't mean for him to leave the barn. No, with a sinking heart he realized she was asking him to leave the farm.

He took a deep, slow breath. "If I've offended you—"

"No, it's not that."

"The neighbors then?" he hazarded. Was she mortified that Mr. Kauffman knew she was entertaining a guest while her father was bedridden? He could set that straight and squelch any rumors. "Sadie, we can explain to people how things were. You don't need to worry about gossip. You've been the model of propriety."

"It's—it's not that."

"What then?"

He waited, but she said nothing. His stomach began to churn with anxiety. Something was terribly wrong, at least from Sadie's perspective. At last he felt he needed to break the silence.

He stepped toward her. "If it's my trying to kiss you that's upset you, please know I didn't mean anything dishonorable by it."

"No, no." She stepped away, toward the barn door. "You've been a true gentleman, Harry. But I can't go on saying one thing and living another. I shan't be eating dinner tonight, so don't wait for me."

His concern changed to alarm, and he followed her out into the barnyard. "What are you talking about? Sadie, tell me what's bothering you so."

She was closing the door without comment.

"Here, let me do that."

She stepped aside, and he drew the heavy door into place. When he turned around, she was walking quickly toward the house. He hurried to catch up with her.

"Sadie, stop, please."

She paused and looked at him in the twilight, and he took that as a good sign. At least she would hear him out.

"Look—I can't leave until I know you're secure again." He

shoved his hands into his pockets so that she wouldn't wonder if he was going to reach for her again, although he longed to do just that. "If it's fair tomorrow, Zeke and I can finish patching the roof, but we need to get the broken windows fixed, too. After that, Zeke can probably go it alone, or he can fetch his older son to help him, the one he told me sometimes helps around here."

"Ephraim." She nodded.

"Well, we ought to get that far within a week. Then I can go and feel peaceful about it."

Her troubled eyes regarded him, and he knew that peace was the last thing he would feel. She wanted him to go. He couldn't help believing the moment in the barn had something to do with that, regardless of what she had said.

❧

The days went too quickly. When Harry awoke each morning, the first thing he did was go outside the little cabin and glare at the rising sun. Rain would serve him far better.

Sadie had kept a cool distance between them since their conversation in the barn, and he was beginning to doubt he had enough time to unravel her reasons. She was polite, and sometimes at dinner he even caught her watching him with what he could only feel was a mournful longing, but she gave him no encouragement. Any suggestion of playful banter was gone, and the spark he had felt jump between them on other occasions was conspicuously absent.

They didn't speak of his leaving again, but they both knew it was imminent. The roof was done, and when the outside walls were patched and the windows replaced, his sojourn at the Spinning Wheel Farm would end.

"One of us had best go to town for the windowpanes," Zeke said one morning, "or else we can't finish the job."

"You go," Harry said. "I'll keep at the sashes while you're gone. I ought to be able to finish the one for the parlor this morning. Then the two for the upstairs windows, and I guess you won't need me anymore."

Zeke eyed him with open curiosity. "You welcome to stay as long as you like, Mr. Harry."

"Thank you. I should get back to my place."

Zeke nodded. "We'll be sorry to see the back of you."

Harry sighed and leaned on the rail fence that edged the pasture beside Zeke's house. "Zeke, I hate to go. I truly do, but I can't stay much longer."

"Why not, Mr. Harry? You like it here."

"I do, but. . .Zeke, you know I've got obligations in Kentucky, and besides, Sadie wants me to go."

"No, suh."

"Yes."

Zeke pulled a dry grass stem and stuck it between his teeth. He glanced at Harry then looked thoughtfully out over the pasture. "Miss Sadie sets a lot of store by you, suh."

Harry shook his head. "Maybe a few days ago, but not now. She's asked me to leave, Zeke."

"I. . .just can't believe it, Mr. Harry."

Harry turned around and leaned back against the rails with a sigh. "I was all primed to speak to her father, you know. I wanted to ask for her hand." He gave Zeke a rueful smile. "Wasn't sure if Mr. McEwan would go along with it, but I had hopes. We got along pretty well last spring. But now. . . well, Sadie pretty much let me know she wouldn't consider it, even if her father would."

"No." Zeke was very quiet, and his frown stretched from his wrinkled forehead to his drooping mouth.

"She's the kind of woman I was hoping for," Harry said with a shrug. "She's prettier than a sunset in Jamaica, and she works hard and doesn't complain. Treats you and Tallie well, too. But besides all that about Sadie, as long as I'm here, I'm keeping your family apart. While Tallie stays up yonder with

Sadie, you have to bach it down here with Pax. No, Zeke, it's time for me to meander."

"Well, I know one thing," Zeke said. "It's time for breakfast now. Grab your hat, suh, and let's get movin'." He stuck his head inside the cabin and shouted, "Pax! Come on, boy! You know your momma won't keep breakfast all day for you."

On their way up to the big house, Pax wrangled with Zeke over the question of the trip to Winchester for the glass.

"I can handle it, Papa. I been to town a thousand times with you or Mr. Oliver. I know what to do. And I can make sure Mr. MacPheters packs the windowpanes so's they won't break on the way back.

"I don't know," Zeke said.

"The boy can do it," Harry said, even though he knew that would leave Zeke here to help him, and the job would be done faster. By supporting Pax, he was shortening his stay.

Sadie didn't appear at breakfast while he was in the kitchen with Zeke and Pax, and Harry assumed she was with Oliver. Tallie went upstairs and came back a few minutes later with money for the glass.

"You'd best go with the boy," she told Zeke. "Miss Sadie say Mr. MacPheters might want cash, and Pax ain't never carried this much before. Besides, if the boy break the windows, she be out her money."

"I suppose," Zeke said.

Harry said nothing, but when Zeke told Pax to go to the barn and prepare the wagon, Harry pulled the boy aside just behind the lean-to.

"Pax, while you and your pa are at the store, can you do a little errand for me?"

"Oh, yes, suh." Pax's dark eyes shone as Harry drew a handful of coins from his pocket.

"You get yourself some candy, and I want something pretty for Miss Sadie and your momma. I want to thank them for letting me stay so long, you see."

Pax nodded, staring at Harry all the while. "What kind of pretties, suh?"

"Oh, maybe some new gloves?"

Pax's brow furrowed.

"Ask your papa," Harry said. "If he thinks that's too personal, he'll know what to get."

Zeke came out the back door and scowled at Pax. "You ain't got the wagon ready?"

"My fault," said Harry.

"I'm doin' Mr. Harry's business, Pa." Pax drew himself up with importance.

"Well, git on to the barn now and do your own business." Zeke drew his arm back as if he would swat the boy, and Pax ran for the barn, but Harry knew it was all a show.

"Zeke, I really, really need to talk to Mr. Oliver," Harry said.

Zeke shook his head sorrowfully. "I wish you'd quit askin' me, suh. I just can't let you. If anything bad should happen, Miss Sadie wouldn't forgive us."

Harry sighed. "Just how bad is he, Zeke? Tell me the truth now."

Zeke's mouth worked for a few seconds, and he glanced at Harry then looked down toward the barn. "Well, suh, he's bad. Real bad."

"But Sadie spends a good part of the day with him every day, and you told me she talks to him."

"Yes, suh. Miss Sadie talks to her Father every single day. That's a fact."

"Does Oliver talk back?" Zeke wouldn't meet his gaze, and Harry pressed further. "Well, Zeke, what I don't understand is how your boss can be so very ill that he can't even see me in his bedroom once in a week's time, and yet you claim he's talking to his daughter about business and such all the time."

Zeke drew himself up and looked him in the eye with the air of a martyr. "I can assure you, suh, that Miss Sadie receives guidance from her Father every day on how to run the farm."

Harry shook his head, at a loss to comprehend the situation. All he knew was that he wanted some sort of permission from Oliver McEwan to pay his addresses to his daughter. Surely if she knew she had her father's approval, Sadie would agree. Harry couldn't forget the sweetness of her embrace before she had torn away from him that night in the barn. For a few seconds it had been the culmination of his dream. He realized that since May it had been in the back of his mind. If Sadie lived up to his memories of her, he had intended to speak to her father about marrying her. He tried to keep his exasperation in check as he told Zeke, "I would really like to see Oliver before I go, if only for a few minutes. You know that, don't you?"

"That's impossible. I'm sorry, but it can't be done."

Harry pulled his felt hat off and dashed it to the ground. "Zeke, I'm losing my patience. I can't understand how Oliver can be giving Sadie so much help if he's too sick to see a client, even in his bedroom. You know what I want to talk to him about, don't you? And I don't mean horses."

Zeke stared down at Harry's dirty hat. "Yes, suh, I reckon I do."

"That's right, you do. I want to speak to him about Sadie, to see if he'd be averse to me courting her. You don't have a reason to keep that from happening, do you, Zeke? Do you have something against me?"

Zeke looked up at him with wide eyes. "Oh, no, suh. I like you fine, Mr. Harry, and I think you'd be a wonderful husband for Miss Sadie. But you told me yourself, she give you the broom."

Harry heaved a sigh and tried once more to reason it out. "But it's her father's illness that's holding her back, don't you see? It's got to be that. I know she cares for me." He stared at Zeke. "Has anyone actually told Oliver I want to see him? Does he even know I'm here, Zeke?"

Zeke stooped and picked up the hat. He dusted it off and handed it to Harry. "I'm truly sorry, suh. It ain't going to happen."

Harry stared at him for a long moment. Maybe he should just march upstairs and go to Oliver's room and ask him. But, no, he couldn't override Sadie's wishes so blatantly. She would surely be angry then. Or would she? Maybe she would be relieved if he took the initiative and forced the issue.

Harry pulled in a deep breath, realizing his feelings for Sadie were keeping him from looking at the situation rationally. His hostess had asked him to leave as soon as possible. He couldn't disrespect that. It wasn't in his nature, and it wouldn't win him favor with Sadie if he acted that way. He put on his hat and headed for the lean-to where he had laid out the wood needed to repair the window sashes.

nine

Sadie stuck out her tongue and squinted in fierce concentration. Harry and Zeke were fitting the new window into Tenley's bedroom, and Harry had entrusted her with putting the glass panes in the second frame, for the room next to her brother's. She bent over a makeshift worktable the men had set up in the front yard—two sawhorses supporting a couple of planks that held the window.

The work was exacting, as Sadie had to fit the panes to the wooden sash Harry had built to replace the one that was crushed. She inserted tiny glazier's points on the outside of the glass to hold each pane in place then applied the putty carefully to seal each pane to the wooden frame. Then she had to wipe away the excess before it dried, leaving the windows clear and sparkling.

Harry had done a good job, and the spaces were precisely the right size. Her task was tedious, rather than creative, but she was determined to do it well.

Of course, when these two windows were in place, Harry would be leaving. He had saved her a lot of money by making it unnecessary to hire a skilled carpenter. The parlor window was finished. If she hadn't known better she'd have thought it was the old one, but Harry had totally rebuilt it. It had taken him three days to do it right.

The smaller bedroom sashes hadn't demanded as much time, but still Harry had been here two weeks now.

Sadie thought her heart would break when he finally left, but even so she looked forward to the relief his departure would bring. The strain between them was almost unbearable.

Zeke and Pax had come home from Winchester with the windowpanes a few days ago, bearing candy, a colorful new head scarf for Tallie and several spools of fine lace and ribbon for Sadie. She had begun to scold Zeke for spending her scarce resources on trifles, but Pax had cried, "It was Mr. Harry's money, Miss Sadie. He paid for your pretties."

She nearly lost control then and had to flee to her room so no one would see her weep. Harry was too dear. In the middle of her agony and sorrow, he bought treats for her poor friends and showered her with fancy trimmings.

"There will be better days," he told her that evening at dinner when she thanked him. "You'll feel like sewing again. I know you love to design pretty clothes, and Zeke thought you'd enjoy those gifts sometime when things are looking better."

At that moment, she'd almost wished she had worn the green gown. She knew Harry wanted to see her in it, and she wanted to see his reaction when she wore the dress with its intricate stitching.

I can't encourage him, she reminded herself. It seemed so unfair. They could have had such lovely times together.

She bent over the window sash where it rested on the sawhorses. Now and then she glanced toward the house where the men were working. Zeke had stood the tall ladder against the side of the house and mounted it. She couldn't help looking up to where Harry was leaning out Tenley's window, steadying the sash as Zeke fitted it into the frame. They had torn out and replaced the broken lumber around the window, and now the new one was almost in position. Pax stood below, bracing the ladder.

A sudden shout from Zeke made her look up, just in time to see the heavy window frame falling.

"Pax!" Sadie screamed.

The boy jumped back away from the ladder, but the corner

of the window caught him on the head, and he crumpled to the ground as the glass shattered around him.

"Pax!" Zeke scrambled down the shaking ladder. Sadie ran toward them. Harry had the presence of mind to lean out the window hole and grasp the top of the ladder to keep it from sliding to the side. As soon as Zeke reached the ground, Harry let go and disappeared from the window.

Zeke huddled over his son, moaning, "My boy, my boy."

Sadie reached his side. "How bad is it, Zeke?"

"He bleedin' bad, Miss Sadie. He got a big gash on the side of his head, and his arm's bleedin'."

"The glass got him," she said.

Harry came tearing out the front door and hopped over the side railing of the porch, landing a few feet from the ladder.

"Be careful." Sadie straightened and held up her hands. "There's glass everywhere, Harry. Stay back."

Zeke picked up the boy and carried him out away from the side of the house, laying him tenderly on the grass. "He's breathin', Mr. Harry. What do we do?"

"We need to stop the bleeding. But be careful. If there's glass in his cuts, we don't want to push it in deeper." Harry looked at Sadie. "Can you get us something to bandage him with?"

As Sadie turned, Tallie charged around the corner of the house. "What happened? What's all the ruckus?"

She stopped as she saw Pax's prone form then turned her eyes heavenward. "Oh, dear Jesus! Help us now!"

"Where's the nearest doctor?" Harry asked.

"I done told you—they ain't a doctor," Zeke said grimly. "If they was, we'd have had him here for Mr. Oliver when he needed him."

"Oh, Lawd, oh, Lawd!" Tallie wailed, clasping her hands together. "My baby! Save my baby boy!"

Sadie ran to her and put her arms around her. "Come, Tallie. We can pray while we fetch what's needed. I'll get some hot water and clean linen. You fix my bed so they can bring him there."

"Not in your bed, Miss Sadie. It ain't right."

"Well, that's what we're doing."

"Where will you sleep tonight?" Tallie asked.

"We'll worry about that later. Now do as I say!"

Tallie blinked at her then lifted her skirt and ran for the front door. Sadie followed, shouting to Harry, "As soon as you can move him, take him up to my bedchamber!"

❧

At midnight Tallie sat by her son's bedside, humming a dolorous hymn. Harry stepped softly into the room, and Tallie said, "You sleep, Miss Sadie. I want to stay with him."

"Tallie, it's me."

She jumped and turned to look at him.

"I thought I'd sit awhile with the boy."

"Bless you, Mr. Harry. You don't have to do that. I won't be able to sleep anyhow."

Harry felt tears threaten him as he looked down at the boy's angelic, dark face, still against the snowy pillow, but he smiled at her. "I guess this is a mother's post."

"That it is."

"I just wanted to help, Tallie."

"I know. I know."

He saw a straight chair before Sadie's secretary and pulled it over beside the rocker Tallie occupied. "If I'd only kept a better hold on that window. I'm so sorry, Tallie."

"It ain't your fault, Mr. Harry. Don't you be a-thinkin' that way."

"I can't help it."

"It was my Zeke dropped the window."

"No, you mustn't blame him. It was me, too. Both of us lost our hold."

Tallie was silent for a minute. "I don't blame neither of you."

Harry bit his upper lip. Better she feel that way than to have her blaming her husband. He would say no more on the subject.

"Where did you put Miss Sadie?" he asked, and Tallie glanced at him.

"She in her brother's old room. She put the bed back together in there herself."

Harry nodded. "I didn't know but she might have a cot in her father's room."

"No, no, she'll sleep better where she is."

"I think Pax will be better tomorrow, Tallie. I truly do."

"I hope so, Mr. Harry."

Harry stretched out his long legs and leaned back with a sigh. "I'm sure he's concussed, but the skull wasn't broken."

"That good or bad?"

"I think it's good. We'll know more when he regains consciousness."

"Them big words." Tallie shook her head.

"If he comes to, we'll know," Harry said.

"Will you pray for him?"

"Of course. I have been already since the minute it happened." Harry reached for her hand, and Tallie squeezed his fingers.

"I'm glad you're a prayin' man. We need a lot of prayer just now."

Harry bowed his head and earnestly sought the Lord's mercy for Pax. He'd spent two weeks living with this boy and his father, and the family was precious to him now. He'd had enough conversations with young Pax to know the condition of his heart.

"Dear Lord," he prayed aloud, "you know this brother in Christ is in need. We ask for Your will, Father. We know that if You should take him home now, he'd be in a wonderful place with You. But his momma and his pa would be devastated,

Lord, and we beg You to spare Pax's life. Give him health and strength again so Tallie and Zeke won't have to worry about him. And we pray for Mr. Oliver, too, Lord. Please help him to regain his health."

Tallie began to sob, and Harry said quickly, "Amen."

"Amen." Tallie blew her nose on a square of calico.

"Are you all right?" he asked, leaning toward her.

"Yes, suh. I be as good as I can be."

"Can I do anything for you? Maybe I could check Mr. Oliver—"

"No!"

Harry was startled, but Tallie patted his arm. "It's best to leave him be."

"If you're sure he's resting. Isn't there anything else I can do, Tallie?"

She shook her head. "You'd best sleep, suh. In the mornin' you can fetch my older son to come and see his brother. And, like you say, maybe things be better in the mornin'."

❧

Sadie lay awake, staring at the canvas that covered the hole where the window should have been. She could have spent the night in her father's room, but somehow she'd known that sleep would elude her in that chamber. Why she'd imagined she would find it here in Tenley's room, she had no idea.

They had to end this charade. Harry had done nothing to deserve the shabby treatment they had given him. The irony was that Harry himself would say they had been kind to him. The knowledge of their deception and of the lies she herself had tacitly told made her physically ill. Even Tallie was ignoring the little things Zeke let fall that implied Sadie's father would be up and about again one day. The dear servant's loyalty to her mistress was causing Tallie to go against her honest nature, and that grieved Sadie.

Harry's compassion for Pax when the boy was injured had

touched her deeply. Sadie knew Harry blamed himself for the accident. He was becoming like family to Zeke and Tallie, and now he felt he had let them down. He had injured their son, perhaps fatally. That was the way Harry saw it. Sadie wished she could take that sickening guilt away for him.

"Dear Lord, I care too much about him," she whispered in the dark. "You've got to take him away from here. I fear I'm past beginning to love him. Lord, please, if You have a way for us to straighten this out, show us now. Otherwise, what can I do but send him away believing a lie?"

If only she had told him everything from the start. But that would have meant betraying Zeke's deception. They had all thought it was only for a day and it wouldn't matter, but now it had gone so far that Sadie didn't see a way to make it right without hurting several people.

The last two weeks had opened up a new world for her as she got to know Harry. Tallie said they had seen the stuff he was made of. Sadie didn't want to think about how bleak her life would be when Harry left. If only she had the courage to tell him, even now, and face whatever came. Rejection? Anger? Condemnation? Could she take that from Harry? It was too dire to contemplate. Tears left the corners of her eyes and streaked down her face to her ears.

I'm so tired of crying, dear Father. I've lost Tenley and Papa, and now I'm losing Harry. Please, don't take Pax away from us, too.

ten

Sadie lingered in her room before dinner, wondering again if she was making a huge mistake. In the three days since Pax's injury, the boy had made a marvelous recovery. He was back in the little cabin with Zeke and Harry now and today had even gone back to helping feed the horses and performing his barn chores.

Sadie had her own bedroom back, and her daily routine seemed more normal. The windows were finished—Harry had gone to town himself for more glass the day after the accident while Tallie and Zeke hovered over Pax.

This would be their last dinner together. Harry had no reason to stay on now; the outside repairs were done, and Pax was on the mend.

She knew he didn't want to leave, and she didn't want that either. The things she had learned about Harry in the last few days only confirmed what she already knew. He was witty, intelligent, diligent, and compassionate. Her love for him had blossomed, and yet she'd kept it in check out of necessity.

But now, on this final evening together, she had made a momentous decision. She would wear the velvet gown.

Was that foolish?

Dinnertime arrived, but still she hesitated, wondering if she should go down in the dress she loved. If only her mother were there to advise her! She stared into the mirror. Her auburn hair gleamed in the lamplight, and her eyes were huge. They picked up the color of the dress and seemed more green than blue this evening. She had added an extra row of lace at the cuffs and neckline from the trimmings Harry had paid for. She wasn't sure he would notice it, but that was all right. She wanted to be wearing something that he had given her tonight. The dress suited her. For once she did not think she looked gawky and immature. Would Harry see her as. . . beautiful?

Her conscience told her she was a fool. This was no way to send a man packing. The conflict in her heart was clouding her reasoning. She should put on her dowdiest housedress and treat him with cool courtesy tonight and not go downstairs in the morning until he had gone.

But she knew she couldn't do that. And here she was, wearing the gown he had requested that she wear a week ago.

Before she could change her mind, she strode from the room and down the stairs.

Harry rose when she entered the parlor, and his eager smile sent a thrill through her. His eyes glowed as he took her hands.

"Sadie, you look wonderful."

Her lips trembled as she gazed up at him. All she could get out was a whispered "Thank you."

Dinner was a bit strained at first, but Zeke and Tallie livened things up. They insisted on serving the two in the dining room as they did every evening. They were on familiar terms with Harry now, and Zeke soon had them both laughing with his comments. Tallie's motherly instincts were at the forefront.

"You eat up, Mr. Harry. You got a long trip ahead of you tomorrow." She brought the platter of meat to him, her meaning unmistakable. If Harry didn't take seconds, she would be insulted.

"Yes, Tallie. I'll miss your scrumptious cooking." He speared a slab of roast beef with the serving fork.

Tallie looked at her husband. "Zeke, get some hot gravy for Mr. Harry."

"This is fine," Harry said, reaching for the china gravy boat, but Zeke snatched it up before he could lift it.

"Oh, no, Mr. Harry. That gravy's cold. You need hot gravy for my Tallie's biscuits and roast beef."

He hurried toward the kitchen. Harry looked at Sadie and shrugged, his eyes twinkling. "I'll miss the service, too."

"Spoiled you, have we?" Sadie asked.

"I'll say. Things were never like this on board ship."

"You got people to look after you in Kentucky?" Tallie asked.

Harry's eyebrows shot up. "You mean. . .family?"

"Slave folks."

"No, Tallie, I don't. No kinfolk there, either."

"Well, what you want to live in Kentucky for?" Tallie shook her head.

When they were alone in the parlor half an hour later, Sadie's nerves assailed her. She sat in a chair, and Harry paced the room slowly, examining all the paintings once more and touching the knickknacks on the mantel.

"I am glad we have this evening together," Harry said, staring down into the empty fireplace, not looking at her.

"So am I."

He turned and smiled at her. "That gown is magnificent on you. Thank you for wearing it."

"You're welcome." Sadie swallowed hard. There were many things she wished to say, but she wasn't sure she could voice any of them. When she inhaled, her chest hurt, so she kept quiet.

Harry went to the settee and sat down facing her. "Sadie, I want to tell you how much I've enjoyed my stay here."

"Oh, that's. . .there's no need."

He shook his head. "You've been wonderful, all of you."

"Harry, we should be thanking you for staying. You've helped us in so many ways!"

He sighed. "I hate to leave, but I know the time has come.

Sadie, I can't go without telling you how much I admire you."

She shifted uneasily in her chair. This was what she wanted to hear, but it only brought more turmoil to her heart. He admired her! And yet she was a lying hypocrite.

Harry went on quickly. "I know you're a modest woman, but your faithfulness and tenacity are undeniable. I've seen how much this farm means to you. You've run it admirably, even during this time of stress and illness. Your family—and I'm including Zeke and Tallie and Pax in that—comes first with you. I believe you've broken my heart because of that, and I'm not sure why."

Sadie caught her breath and stared down at the figured carpet. "Harry, I never meant to hurt you."

"I know that. I just wish you could be open with me and tell me all your troubles. I can only think I could help you change things."

Sadie felt a crushing weight on her chest. If only she could do that! He might be right—so far he'd been right about most things. Maybe if she told him now, he could help her with the legal and social morass she knew would envelop her soon.

A montage of images flashed through her mind. It was possible she could be evicted from her family home. She might be forced to flee, penniless and without hope, and be separated from her beloved family servants. The thing that frightened her most, the one she didn't dare mention even to Tallie, was that she might be arrested. Yes, she and Zeke and Tallie might all be charged with. . .something, she wasn't sure what, but a vague certainty that they had broken multiple laws of the Commonwealth lurked in the back of her mind.

Harry left his seat and knelt beside her chair.

"You must know that I love you."

She drew in a shaky breath and avoided looking at him. If she gazed into those earnest brown eyes, she would be lost.

She felt his warm, strong hand cover hers.

"Sadie, tell me you love me, too."

As she struggled for her answer, tears welled in her eyes. He slid his arm around her.

"Sadie, dearest, look at me."

Slowly she turned her head. "Harry." It was all she could get out, and even that was a little squeak. Her heart raced, and his melting brown eyes had the effect she'd known they would have.

"I'm going to do one of three things," Harry said.

"What?" she managed.

"Either I'm going to run up those stairs and speak to your father—"

"No! You mustn't."

Harry frowned. "All right then." He took a deep breath. "All right, I'm going to do one of two things. Either I'm going to kiss you, or you're going to tell me to leave now, and I won't see you again."

She stared at him.

"Sadie?"

"I. . ."

"It's up to you."

"I don't want you to leave, but—"

Harry didn't wait for her to finish. He drew her up out of her chair, and his lips found hers. Sadie tensed for an instant. Had she given the wrong answer?

No, her heart told her. *You love him. This is the right thing.*

She let him draw her closer, reveling in the joy his touch brought her. It was far beyond her expectations or imaginations, and she wanted the moment to last forever. He held her in his arms and showered soft kisses along her temple, to the corner of her eye.

"Sadie, I love you so much."

She gulped for air, knowing that all she needed to say was two words: *Don't leave.*

And then what? Would he be embroiled in their troubles, too? Or would he betray them when he found out the truth? The joy that had flooded her a moment ago was overcome by guilt, and she pushed him away reluctantly.

"Harry, we mustn't. You know my father is. . ." She sobbed. "His condition is very serious."

"Yes. Yes, I know."

"I do love you, Harry, but—" As triumph leaped into his eyes, she pressed her hands against the front of his shirt to keep him from sweeping her into his embrace again. "But that doesn't change anything."

"I don't understand. It should change everything."

She sighed. "Please respect my wishes. You need to leave in the morning. That's the way it is right now. There are things I have to face on my own."

He studied her face, and Sadie made herself return his gaze. Her heart hammered, and she longed to nestle against his chest again and feel safe, but that would be a false security.

At last he stood back, his head bowed. "All right. I've done everything I know how to do. But tell me, Sadie. If I were to come back, say in the spring, would things be different?"

Her heart lurched. She hadn't considered this possibility. Would she even be here next spring?

"Sadie?"

"It's. . .possible." She looked up at him. He was smiling. He grasped her hands and lifted them to his lips.

"In the spring, then, when the mountains are passable."

❧

Harry went to the barn with Zeke and Pax at dawn to tend the livestock. While the father and son fed the horses, Harry tied his pack to the cantle of his saddle and gave Pepper a grooming.

His heart was heavy. He didn't want to ride back to Kentucky and leave Sadie behind. He would spend all winter pining for her. She had admitted she loved him. He smiled at that. It was a start, but her father needed her here. Harry was certain now that it was Oliver's health that was weighing her down. She didn't feel she could make a commitment to him while her father was so ill, and she felt bound to the farm and her family.

Harry sighed and fastened a lead rope to Pepper's halter. Maybe he was too aggressive last night, but at least it had brought a declaration from her. He could live all winter on that if he had to. She loved him. She wasn't as ready to start a new life as he was. He could wait. He didn't know what would come of it in the future, but one thing he knew for sure: He couldn't ride off and forget her. He would hold the memory of Sadie in his heart all winter and come back in the spring to see if she was ready for his suit.

"You sure you'll be all right alone with those mares, Mr. Harry?" Pax asked him, leaning against a post between the stalls.

Harry smiled. Pax would love it if he offered to take him with him to Kentucky. He wouldn't mind the company himself, but he was sure the boy would get homesick before they left the Shenandoah Valley, and Tallie wouldn't abide the idea of her youngest leaving home so early. Harry had learned that all four of her daughters lived at least a day's ride away, and only Pax and his married brother, Ephraim, were close enough now for Tallie to spoil them. No, she wouldn't let the youngest go easily.

"I'll be fine, Pax. They're well-behaved horses. You folks have taught them good manners."

"You gonna lead them all, suh?"

"Most likely your pa will help me tie the lead ropes into a string. I don't expect much trouble."

"What if a Injun tries to steal them while you're sleepin' at night?"

"Not too many Indians left where I'm headed, son. You'd have to go a little farther west for that."

Pax was disappointed, he could tell.

"How's your head feel?" Harry asked.

"Fine, suh. Pa said I could ride today."

Harry nodded. "Glad to hear it. You be good now and help your pa get things ready for winter."

Pax scuffed his toe in the straw on the barn floor. "Yes, suh. We gonna miss you."

"I'll miss you, too." He ruffled the boy's woolly hair. "You want to take Pepper to the water trough for me?"

Pax grinned and hurried to take Pepper out into the barnyard. Harry followed him. He took a deep breath and looked toward the house. Would Sadie show herself this morning? He'd promised Tallie he'd eat breakfast in the kitchen before leaving.

A flash of color caught his eye, and he saw a figure disappearing among the trees at the side of the house toward the river, beyond the vegetable garden. It was a slender woman in a full mulberry-colored skirt. It had to be Sadie!

He stepped forward eagerly then thought to call to Pax, "Just put him away when he's finished drinking. I'll see you at breakfast."

Pax waved his acknowledgment, and Harry hurried toward where he had seen her. He found a narrow path, leading between the apple trees and beyond. He followed it and mounted a gentle knoll. At its crest he stopped in surprise. A burial plot lay on the south slope, overlooking the river. Perhaps twenty stone grave markers were in it, and a rough rail fence bounded the area. In the middle, kneeling before a wooden cross, was Sadie.

eleven

Harry squinted at the headstone nearest her. Her mother's grave. Then what was the cross beside it for? They had only learned of Tenley's death a few weeks ago. Zeke and Sadie had both spoken of the letter Oliver received from Tenley's commander. Neither had said a word about his remains being received. Surely Sadie's brother couldn't be buried here in Virginia.

But the earth where she knelt was just growing up in tender grass, and he could see that the grave was much newer than Mrs. McEwan's.

The obvious truth broke on him, but Harry refused to believe it. Against his will, the many comments Zeke had dropped flooded his memory.

Mr. Oliver is resting. Mr. Oliver wasn't disturbed by the storm. Mr. Oliver is no better today, but no worse.

It couldn't be. Sadie wouldn't lie to him so blatantly. He tried to recall the things she had said about her father, and suddenly he was sure. Her statements that she couldn't go on living as she was, and her cryptic remark about saying one thing and living another. . .it all made sense now.

He wanted to go to her, but the incredulity he felt brought on a heavy dread. Did he really want to know the truth? That would mean confronting the woman he loved. Harry didn't want to accuse people he had believed to be his closest friends of lying to him. But then, wasn't that why she hadn't told him? She didn't want to face that kind of chaos, either. Perhaps they would all be better off if he left without saying a word.

He needed time to think. He started to turn away, wondering if he could escape without Sadie knowing he had seen her, but at that moment she rose and turned around.

She gasped and clutched her hands together at her breast, staring at him. Her lips were parted, and the anguish he saw in her eyes stabbed through the dull pain that had encased him.

She knew he had figured it out; his expression must have revealed it. There was no way to make her believe otherwise. Harry wished he weren't so transparent.

He took a few steps forward, and she met him at the low gate.

"Why didn't you tell me?" he whispered.

She swallowed hard then caught a ragged breath. She looked at him then away. "Tell you what?"

Anger spouted up inside him so suddenly that it shocked him. "Oh, stop it, Sadie. Your father's dead. He's been dead for weeks, hasn't he? If anyone had told me you would do this, I'd have called him out. You are the last person on earth I would expect to lie to me, the very last." He ignored the tears in her eyes. "I begged you to tell me what was wrong. Why, Sadie? Why couldn't you trust me?"

She dashed tears from her eyes with one hand. "I wanted to, but I was so afraid."

"Afraid of me?"

"We didn't know you well, not at first. How could I tell if you were trustworthy? I'd only met you once."

"Why should that matter? Sadie, I heard Zeke tell your neighbors your father was alive. What is going on? Why on earth would you try to hide his death? It makes no sense at all."

She sobbed into her hand, turning partly away from him. "When he died, we had to bury him. Ordinarily we'd have sent for the preacher, but the reverend had left shortly before on his circuit. It would have taken Zeke a week or more to catch him. We couldn't wait. It was so hot. We couldn't wait."

She was shaking, and Harry's love for her struggled against the outrage he felt.

"Even so. . ."

"And then we got to worrying about the property. You see, my father had left his estate to Tenley, but with Tenley dead we weren't sure what would happen to us."

Harry frowned. "What do you mean?"

"I. . .Zeke and Tallie and I aren't sure whether I'll be allowed to inherit the farm. Zeke recalled the Widow Scott. When her husband died, their farm went to his cousin's son, and she was turned out. We didn't know what would become of us if I lost the farm, and. . .well, when you came, Zeke said something about Papa, and you thought he meant. . ."

"You should have seen a lawyer."

She shook her head hopelessly. "I don't know any lawyers, Harry. I wouldn't even know where to find one." She looked off downriver. "Washington, maybe? There was no one within several days' journey who could issue a death certificate."

"What do your neighbors do when somebody dies? What did your father do when your mother died?"

"I don't know! I don't know!" She slumped against the low fence, holding on to the top rail and weeping.

"I can't believe you lied about it. Just because you couldn't get a doctor or a preacher—" Harry shook his head as if to clear the cobwebs. "I can't believe you all conspired against me. Even Pax? I love that kid. How could he not spill it to me?"

Sadie winced. "Pax is very loyal to this family."

"But Tallie. There's not a dishonest bone in her body."

"We were afraid, Harry. We wanted to tell you. Tallie has been distraught over this, but we were afraid."

"I would never do anything to hurt you."

"We didn't know that then. Don't you see? When you arrived, we thought it was just for a day, and Zeke thought it would be best to say nothing and let you assume Papa was ill. We didn't know but what you'd tell someone, and the law would come and evict us all. But when you stayed and we got to know you, it was too late. We couldn't tell anyone then that he was dead. How would that look? It just got worse and worse the longer you stayed, even though we were thankful you came, and we. . .grew to love you." She hid her face then, sobbing uncontrollably.

"What you did was foolish, Sadie." It came out more harshly than he'd intended, and she jerked her chin up.

"Don't speak to me in that tone, sir, or I shall have to ask you to leave at once."

He took a deep breath. "No need. I was just leaving anyway."

He walked quickly over the knoll and through the orchard. The confusion in his mind was nearly as painful as the sorrow in his heart. He ought to be holding her in his arms this moment, but he couldn't make himself turn back. She had lied to him, not once, but many times. He'd thought he knew her, but apparently not.

Pax was still holding Pepper near the water trough, and Zeke stood with him, anxiously watching Harry approach.

"Mr. Harry, everythin' all right?" Zeke asked. Harry thought his grin was a little strained.

"Bring my saddle, please." Harry clipped out the words, and he could tell by the way Zeke's face fell that he knew the ruse was over.

"Yes, suh. Right away." Zeke hurried into the barn, and Pax stood staring at Harry with wide eyes.

"You leavin' us now, Mr. Harry?"

"Yes, Pax."

They stood in uneasy silence until Zeke came from the barn carrying Pepper's tack.

Zeke kept his eyes lowered. "Please don't go off in a tear,

Mr. Harry. It started out all innocent. We didn't mean to—"

"Zeke, I've lived with you for more than a fortnight. We're as close as brothers, or so I thought. But you still don't trust me." Harry seized the saddle blanket and tossed it onto Pepper's back. Pepper snorted and sidestepped, and Harry placed his hand on the gelding's shoulder. "Easy now." If he didn't calm himself, Pepper would fidget all morning. He smoothed the blanket then gently settled the saddle over the withers.

"Just tell me, who buried Oliver?"

Zeke sniffed and kicked at a pebble. "I did, suh. I dug the grave. Then we all. . . It was hard for Miss Sadie, suh, but I made a box in the barn here, and we. . .we said some words and sung the doxology."

"You couldn't have got a few neighbors together to give him a respectful funeral?" Harry made himself stand still and breathe deeply. His anger was resurfacing.

Zeke glanced at Pax then said quietly, "We was afraid what would happen to Miss Sadie if people found out he was gone, suh."

"So Sadie told me. Did you expect to hide it forever?"

Zeke had no answer. He and Pax watched in silence as Harry tightened the cinch strap. He took the halter off Pepper and handed it to Pax then slipped the bridle over Pepper's ears. The bit slid into the horse's mouth, and Harry worked at the buckle. Pax stood twisting the lead rope in his hands.

"Mr. Harry, don't leave like this," Zeke pleaded.

"Oh, sure. I ought to go into the kitchen and have breakfast first with you all." Harry's laugh was bitter.

Zeke shook his head, and his shoulders drooped. "It's just a pity you came when you did."

Harry refused to consider that remark. He needed to get away from this oppressive place. Without another word, he mounted and pushed Pepper into an extended trot.

❧

Sadie stumbled up the path to the dooryard. Zeke stood with his back to her, watching as Harry's horse trotted down the lane.

"Zeke," she called, and he turned toward her.

"Miss Sadie!"

"He knows, Zeke. Harry knows everything."

"I'm sorry—truly I am." His shoulders slumped. "I wanted to help you, Miss Sadie. When your pa died, I only wanted to protect you."

"I know." She put her hand to her forehead. "I'm so tired. I'm sure things will look better when we've had breakfast."

Zeke leaped to her side. "Let me take you inside. You need to sit."

She took his arm, and they turned toward the house. She could almost read her faithful servant's thoughts. Once again he had failed her. All his efforts to shield her from the consequences of her father's death had come to nothing. Perhaps he'd even hoped that he and Tallie had found a husband for her, a man who would love her and protect her from the legal entanglements brought on by this tragedy, a man they could serve with contentment and pride.

Suddenly Pax raced up from behind them. "Pa! Mr. Harry done forgot his mares! Let me go after him." He would have run for the barn, but Zeke grabbed the back of his shirt and held him in place.

"Pa, we gotta catch him. Let me ride after him." Pax squirmed out of Zeke's hold and turned to face him.

Zeke shook his head. "Let him go, boy. This ain't over."

"But them mares! He paid for 'em."

Zeke nodded with a grim smile. " 'Zactly. Mr. Harry needs to put some distance between us and him for a while, but he'll be back."

"I'm not so sure," Sadie said.

"Oh, he'll be back," Zeke insisted. "Meanwhile, we'll be prayin' that things will turn out right."

"Was he right about us lying, Pa? You said it wasn't lying."

Zeke sighed. "I been wrong about things before, son. Now you go and put Mr. Harry's mares out to grass for today then come for breakfast. I'll see Miss Sadie inside."

Sadie knew Zeke would catch it from Tallie as soon as she found out what had happened. She was certain he would rather stay down at the barn with Pax and let her break the news to his wife. But he held on to her firmly and squared his shoulders as they approached the lean-to.

"It's gonna be all right, Miss Sadie," he said just before opening the kitchen door for her.

"God will help us through this." She brushed away a tear, wondering if she could face Tallie without weeping.

Zeke nodded. "I'm powerful sorry I caused all this."

"It wasn't you. It was all of us. I should have known better. That first day, I should have told him everything and let whatever happened happen." She gulped for air and wiped her eyes again.

"I expect my wife will be hoppin' mad when Mr. Harry don't come to eat her special breakfast."

"I'm not sure I can eat, Zeke. Perhaps I'll go in the front door and up to my room."

Zeke sniffed. "I be very, very sorry, Miss Sadie."

She knew she couldn't leave him alone to broach the subject with Tallie.

twelve

By the time the farm was a mile behind him, Harry's blood had cooled to a simmer. It was early, and the day spread before him, empty and bleak. He rode automatically, letting Pepper choose his footing. Then, as the gelding clopped over a wooden bridge that spanned a placid stream, it struck him: He'd left his brood mares behind.

He pulled up for a moment and looked back. It was downright idiotic of him to forget them, but it had completely slipped his mind. Maybe he should turn around and ride back for them. He could be forty miles on the road by nightfall.

No, best go on to the little town ahead. He wasn't ready to face Sadie again, and he had a feeling he wasn't up to seeing Tallie just now either. Zeke might cringe and humble himself before Harry, but Tallie would do no such thing. She would do anything to protect her mistress; she'd proven that. She'd rake him over the coals but good, and somehow the whole calamity would wind up being Harry's fault. And maybe, in some way, it was.

He decided to take a room for the night in Winchester and see how things looked in the morning. After all, he did pay a large sum of money for those mares. He'd better go back and collect them or have his money back. He knew Sadie needed the money, and he did want the mares, so he'd have to go back. He couldn't see any other solution.

He rode on, ruminating on the events of the morning. Why had they lied to him? While Zeke's explanation made some sense, he still couldn't believe Sadie would go along with the deception. Had she truly been afraid of him?

Harry shook his head. The anger still glowed inside him. He'd have done anything for her. Anything! He'd been starting to dream of relocating his horse breeding operation to the Shenandoah Valley. There was no chance of that now. His heart cried, *I love you, Sadie! How could you not trust me?*

He took Pepper to the livery stable and ambled about the town. His wrath still stewed inside him, but it was less urgent now. By noon he didn't feel angry at all, unless he was angry with himself. He had handled the entire situation badly. His wrath dissipated and was replaced by a painful wound that throbbed every time his thoughts came near it.

As he wandered aimlessly down the dusty streets, he remembered that he'd missed breakfast and set about to find a place to eat. He didn't care if it was a late breakfast or an early dinner; he just wanted something filling. He found a boardinghouse that served meals to travelers, but they wouldn't serve luncheon for two hours yet. His stomach was growling by then, and he gave up and walked back to the inn on the main street. The hurt Sadie had inflicted on him had eased to a mournful sadness so long as he didn't think about her. When he did, it flared up and stabbed his heart once more.

Two men in tattered uniforms were leaving the inn. Their faces were hard, and the taller one glanced warily at him. Harry stepped aside to let them come down the steps and watched them as they started down the road on foot, the way he had come.

A wagon rumbled past, and Harry recognized the driver as the McEwans' neighbor, Mr. Kauffman. He raised his hand in greeting, but Mr. Kauffman didn't see him. Just as well, Harry thought. He didn't feel like having a neighborly visit and explaining why he was in town today.

The uniformed men hailed Mr. Kauffman as his wagon came abreast of them, and he pulled his team up. They talked for a few moments. Kauffman was nodding and gesturing toward the road up the valley. To Harry's surprise the two vagrants climbed into the back of the wagon and rode off with Mr. Kauffman.

Guess they prefer bouncing around in a wagon box to wearing out their shoe leather, Harry thought. He hoped Mr. Kauffman arrived home with his pocketbook intact.

He didn't relish the thought of eating the landlady's nondescript stew again, but by this time he was ravenous, so he turned resolutely toward the door of the inn.

❧

"Sadie, baby, you got to eat somethin'." Tallie sighed when she got no response. She set the tray down on the small table beside her mistress's bed. "I brung you a good chicken soup now and fresh bread and apple tart. You need to nourish yourself, child. You gonna make yourself ill."

All morning Sadie had lain in bed. Occasionally Tallie had heard her weeping, but mostly there was a heavy silence throughout the house.

Tallie left the room in defeat and shuffled across the hall to open the door of Mr. Oliver's bedchamber. Time to get the room aired out and go through the master's things. She would begin cleaning in there this afternoon, and perhaps she could interest Sadie in sorting her father's papers and clothing.

She threw the windows open then went downstairs. When she entered the kitchen, Zeke and Pax peered at her silently.

Tallie shook her head. "She still won't eat."

Zeke sighed. "Maybe she'll perk up tomorrow."

"Mr. Harry will come back tomorrow, won't he, Pa?" Pax's earnest question demanded an answer, but Zeke only shrugged so the boy turned to Tallie. "Ma? Won't he?"

"I don't know, son. I didn't see Mr. Harry when he left, so I don't know how overset he was." She sent her husband an icy glare. "I wasn't there when the arsenal exploded, so to speak, unlike some people. I wasn't the one who let Mr. Harry gallop off in a fine pucker."

"He wasn't gallopin'," Zeke protested, "and he wasn't red-hot mad."

"Oh, you tellin' me he's not upset? Sure. That's why he wouldn't come in and eat my flapjacks." She picked up a big wooden spoon and began to stir the chicken broth.

"Well, he wasn't rantin'." Zeke avoided her scathing gaze.

"So Mr. Harry wasn't put out with you?"

Zeke shrugged. "I didn't say that. He just. . .well, he let me know I went down a notch or three in his respect."

Tallie frowned and shook the wooden spoon at him. "One more hour. One more hour, husband, and he would have rode out of here happy."

Zeke put his fists to his forehead. "I know. I know."

"If you ever tell a lie again, I'll. . .I'll. . ."

Zeke shot a sideways look at Pax and hissed, "Hush now, Tallie. The boy!"

"Is Miss Sadie gonna be all right?" Pax blinked at his mother, and she thought he was holding back tears.

"I don't know. Right now she's feelin' so guilty, she's just crushed. If she don't come out of this soon, she gonna get sick." Tallie set a bowl of hot soup before her husband and dipped up another for Pax.

"He'll come back, and when he does, we'll straighten everythin' out," Zeke said, but Tallie thought he lacked confidence.

When they had eaten and she had cleaned up the kitchen, she left Pax drying the dishes and went back upstairs. Sadie was sitting up in bed, sipping a spoonful of broth.

Relief flooded Tallie's heart, and she hurried to the bedside. "There now! That's a good girl!"

"I knew you'd keep fussing at me if I didn't touch it." The listlessness in her voice still troubled Tallie, but they had made a beginning, and she felt sure Sadie would recover from her crisis.

Tallie pulled the rocking chair over and sat down. "Miss Sadie, you know the Lawd will forgive us if we ask Him to."

Sadie's face screwed up into a grimace. "I've asked Him and asked Him, Tallie, but I still feel guilty."

"There, there." Tallie patted the smooth skin of her forearm. "You got to stop blamin' yourself, child. It was me and Zeke more than you, especially Zeke. And we're all sorry. The Lawd knows it, and when we truly repent He stops rememberin' our foolishness, and we got to, too."

Sadie sniffed. "Thank you, Tallie. I know you're right, but I feel positively filthy. I never did anything like that before. Harry said I lied, and he was right. It was a black, putrid lie."

"Hush, hush. It's all forgiven now."

"But what are we going to do, Tallie? Nothing is solved."

"The Lawd knows, and that's what matters. When Mr. Harry comes back for his horses—"

"I don't want to see him if he does come back!"

Sadie's vehemence sent a wave of apprehension through Tallie. "Why not, child?"

"I can't. I can't look into his big, brown eyes ever again. He trusted us, Tallie, and we deceived him. I let him—" She bit her lip, and the tears started again. "I let him kiss me last night, Tallie, and he said he'd come back in the spring, and I let him go on thinking my father would see him then! It was wicked of me."

There was a timid tap on the door, and Tallie turned toward it. "What you want?"

Pax peeked in at them, his eyes wide in the dim light. "They a man at the door, Ma."

Tallie jumped up. "Is it Mr. Harry?"

Pax shook his head. "No, he all ragged, and he limps. I never saw him before."

Tallie took the bowl from Sadie's hands. "You stay put, and I'll send him away. Don't you worry none. I'll just get rid of this tramp. You rest now."

Sadie lay back on the pillow, and Tallie was satisfied. She went down the stairs with Pax close behind her.

"Where's your pa?" Tallie whispered to the boy.

"Yonder at the barn. He's cleanin' out."

Tallie saw that her son had left the door ajar, but no one was on the porch.

"Where he go?" Pax whispered.

Tallie heard a step behind her and whirled toward the parlor door. A man stood in the doorway to the front room, peering at her. He had a thin, wolfish face, and Tallie's heart began to pound. She noted that his ragged jacket had a military cut, and the tarnished buttons looked official.

She felt like scolding him and tossing him right out, but a sudden thought stopped her. If he was from the army, he might have some word of Mr. Tenley.

She looked him up and down. He was sizing her up with the same shrewdness.

"What you want?" she asked, not bothering to pull out the courteous phrases Sadie's mother had taught her to use with guests.

"I'm here to see Mr. Oliver McEwan," the man replied.

Tallie looked into his eyes. She didn't like what she saw, but she didn't draw back. Her job of protecting Sadie was not done yet, and her caution took over. She straightened her shoulders. Before she had time to think, she opened her mouth.

"Mr. Oliver can't see you today, suh. He's been ill, and he's restin'."

thirteen

"I appreciate you seeing me."

Sadie could smell the filthy man from six feet away. She tried not to let her nose wrinkle. She sat down in one of the parlor chairs and studied him.

"I'm only seeing you because my maid said you'd been to Mexico City."

"That's right, miss. I was in the battle there a year ago." He shook his head. "Seems like another life."

"You. . .fought under General Scott?"

"Yes, miss, and a rough time we had of it."

Sadie nodded. "I didn't get your name."

"Mitchell." He paused. "Sergeant Dan Mitchell."

Sadie noted he wore the cotton summer uniform of the Dragoons, which had no doubt been white once but was now a grubby gray.

"And what brings you here, Sergeant Mitchell?"

"Why, young McEwan, of course."

Sadie swallowed hard. "You are speaking of my brother?"

"If Tenley McEwan was your brother, miss. If you don't mind my saying so, but I see a resemblance. You must be Sadie."

It took her a moment to regain her composure. "You were acquainted with him?"

"Yes, ma'am."

She gestured toward a chair, and he seated himself. "What can you tell me about him?"

Mitchell leaned forward and frowned. "I know this is a difficult time for you, miss, but I wanted to meet your father.

You see, Tenley told me all about him and this place before he. . .passed on."

Sadie caught her breath. "You were with him when he died?"

"Yes, I was. As a matter of fact, without me he might have been left lying on the battlefield and. . .well, he wasn't. I got him to the field hospital afterward. I made sure the doctor saw him, but. . .well, it wasn't enough in the end. I'm sorry. He was a fine young fellow."

Sadie came to a decision. She didn't like this man. He was dirty, he smelled of sweat and beer, and he had a shifty manner, but he had been with her dear brother during the chaotic last weeks of his life. She had lost so much so quickly that her grief left her feeling drained and empty. This man was offering her a glimpse of the void she had felt since Tenley went away to war almost two years ago. She wanted to learn everything she could about her brother's last days, and Dan Mitchell might be the only one who could enlighten her.

"Would you care to stay to dinner, Sergeant?"

A look of awe came over his face. "Why, miss, that's mighty gracious of you. I'd be honored if I weren't so scruffy. I'm afraid I don't have any proper clothes now."

Sadie stood. "My maid will bring you some things. You can bathe in the barn. We have a servant who will fix a bath for you there. I believe my late brother's things might fit you."

He was too smelly to continue the conversation as he was. She would give him dinner, but there she drew the line. She wouldn't have him upstairs in the house. She had no reason to trust him, but she would take a small risk to gain an insight into Tenley's death.

"Why, thank you, miss. And I'm sorry your father's not well."

She went to the hall, and he followed her. She called Pax and told him to take the guest to Zeke in the barn and then return for the clothes and linens Tallie would have ready.

Tallie wouldn't like it, and Sadie couldn't blame her. She was a little afraid of Mitchell herself. But she knew that if she turned him away without hearing his story she would always regret it and wonder what he could have told her.

❧

When Dan Mitchell appeared for dinner, Sadie was pleasantly surprised at the improvement in his appearance. A pang of loss struck her as she noted how well Tenley's clothes fit him. He was shorter than Harry and not so broad through the shoulders. His sandy hair was clean now, and he'd shaved.

Sadie had put on one of her nicer day dresses, knowing her guest would not be sporting evening wear. Tallie and Zeke served them in silence, watching the stranger's every move. Sadie knew Tallie had planted a rolling pin in the sideboard, and Zeke had concealed her father's pistol in a cupboard just inside the kitchen door. They had both scolded her for her hasty invitation.

The longer she conversed with Mitchell, the less she felt their caution was needed. It was true he was roughened by his years of harsh living in the army, but he seemed to have a rudimentary command of the manners acceptable in polite circles, and he was eager to please Sadie.

"I believe you said you helped my brother off the field of battle." As she handed him the plate of biscuits, Sadie was careful not to let any emotion creep into her voice.

"Yes, ma'am. I started to carry him. The carnage was awful that day when we attacked the *presidio*, as I'm sure you've heard. I saw Tenley go down, and I knew if I left him there, he'd either be hit again or he'd bleed to death. As soon as there was a lull in the shooting, I went to move him farther back where we had men to tend the wounded. But just as I hoisted him on my shoulder, I took a musket ball in my leg." Mitchell rubbed his thigh and frowned. "It was a terrible day, miss."

"How did you manage to escape?"

"Well, I went down, but I knew we both had to get out of there. Our troops were pulling back, and if we got left there, we'd be right in the line the Mexes were going to take to try and rout our forces. I decided it was do or die for me and Tenley. I picked him up and hobbled along after our detachment."

Sadie was silent for a moment, considering his tale. Was this man truly a compassionate war hero? "That's quite remarkable. My family owes you its deepest gratitude, Sergeant Mitchell."

He looked at her from hooded eyes. "That's partly why I'm here, Miss McEwan. I don't like to put it to you, but if your father is too ill to give me an audience, I suppose I'll have to put myself on your mercy."

"To what are you referring?" She stared at him with apprehension.

He smiled and tilted his head to one side, reaching for his water glass. "Your brother and I were very close, even before we got to the capital. We slept in the same tent for a while, and we swapped a lot of stories."

Zeke was standing in back of Mitchell near the kitchen door. He was scowling and shaking his head behind the soldier. Sadie ignored him.

"Before we went into that last big battle, he asked me to do him a favor," Mitchell went on. "It's not unusual. Lots of men write letters home before they go into battle or give last messages to their friends."

Sadie caught her breath. "Did Tenley write a letter to us? We received nothing."

"No, ma'am, I'm sorry. I didn't mean to raise your hopes like that. What he did was to ask me, if anything happened to him so's he didn't make it home, to visit his family here in Virginia and tell his father how it was at the end."

Sadie felt tears prick her eyes, but when she looked toward the sideboard and caught Tallie's eye, Tallie was frowning.

"I appreciate your making the journey here, sir," Sadie said. "Where are you from? It must have been an inconvenience for you to seek us out."

"Well, miss, I'm not really from anywhere. I was born in Connecticut, they tell me, but then my folks moved to Pennsylvania. After they died, I drifted around here and there, seeing the country and taking jobs where I could. I've been to Georgia, Ohio, and New Jersey, and everywhere in between. Then one day I joined the army, and, well, I got to see a lot more country." He shook his head ruefully. "This here is heaven compared to Mexico, I'll tell you. You don't want to plan a pleasure trip down there."

"The officer who wrote us said Tenley survived several weeks at the hospital in Mexico City."

"Yes, that's correct. At first I thought he'd get better, but he kept going downhill."

"You were close by and saw him while he was being nursed?"

"Yes, ma'am. I spent a few weeks in the hospital myself. It was a big building near the palace, and they'd commandeered it for medical purposes. You see, my wound got infected. The heat and bugs down there are awful, and I think more men died of sickness and infections than from their wounds."

Sadie felt slightly nauseous, and she raised her napkin to her lips. "I'm pleased you recovered," she murmured.

"Yes, well, while I was there I was able to see Tenley every day. He talked to me a lot before he got feverish."

She nodded expectantly, and he went on.

"Your brother told me a lot of things about his family, miss, and one thing he told me was how generous his father was."

Mitchell swabbed the gravy from his plate with half a biscuit and took a large bite. Sadie sipped her tea, grateful he was waiting until he finished chewing before continuing his story.

"The last time I saw him alive, he was in dire straits. He knew he wasn't going to make it."

Sadie winced but could not tell him to stop. She wanted to know everything, every scrap, no matter how painful the knowledge was.

"He told me. . ." Mitchell smiled at her suddenly. "He talked a lot about his daddy. He told me if I ever needed help, to find Oliver McEwan. He said his father would help out a friend of his son's."

He paused, apparently assigning great significance to these words. Sadie waited, certain there was more to come.

"If I ever needed a job or a loan or maybe a letter of reference, his father would help me out, he said."

"I see." She looked at Tallie and Zeke. Both were staring in disapproval at the back of Mitchell's head. "Zeke, perhaps you could serve us coffee in the parlor." Sadie rose, and Mitchell jumped up.

"That sounds lovely, Miss McEwan. Might I be so bold as to ask if you can offer anything stronger?"

She stared at him in embarrassed shock. His manners were less polished than she'd thought.

He added hastily, "My wound, you know. It bothers me some."

"We do not keep spirits in the house, sir. Now, if you would excuse me for a moment, Zeke will show you to the parlor."

Sadie pushed through the door to the kitchen and waited for Tallie to join her.

"You got to get that fellow out of here," were Tallie's first words as she entered carrying two serving dishes. "It's plain he wants more than a fine dinner and some of your brother's cast-off clothes."

"That's unkind, Tallie," Sadie said. She looked toward the

window and saw that it was nearly full dark outside. "It's getting late."

"Yes, but—" Tallie set the dishes down and placed her hands on her hips. "You not thinkin' of lettin' him stay here tonight?"

Sadie shrugged. "I don't like him, but he was kind to Tenley when he needed help."

"Maybe he was and maybe he wasn't."

"What do you mean?"

"You want my opinion? Anybody could say someone told them such and such, just to make folks feel sympathy."

"But he obviously knew Tenley. He knew my name."

"Oh, and he couldn't pry that out of the person who told him where the house was?"

Sadie frowned. She felt a strong discomfort in Mitchell's presence, but she didn't like Tallie implying she was naive. "You're too skeptical, Tallie. He's a veteran who needs a boost."

"Humph! He's a bad egg what needs a kick in the pants. He wants your papa to give him a job, that or some money."

"You may be right, but what can I do? I wasn't the one who told him Papa was ill now, was I?"

"No, but it's a good thing I was the one to see him first. If you'd blurted out the truth with this one, he'd have seen a golden opportunity, and I mean golden. He'd be calculatin' how to get this property away from a simple little orphan girl. Right now he's just expectin' a little silver."

"That's enough, Tallie."

Zeke entered the kitchen just then, and Tallie pounced on him.

"What you want to leave that grifter alone in the parlor for? He'll be pocketin' Miss Sadie's valuables."

"He asked me to get his coffee right away."

"I just bet he did," Tallie said. "He wants a chance to look things over again."

"All right, I'll go tell him you're gettin' it." Zeke pushed the door open.

"Wait, Zeke!" Sadie held herself tall. "I would like Sergeant Mitchell to stay at your house tonight."

"What? No! That bum? He's not sleepin' in my cabin."

"But I thought—well, I can't have him here under the circumstances," Sadie faltered. "I thought perhaps he could stay with you one night. You know, like Harry Cooper did."

Zeke shook his head. "Don't go comparin' that man and Mr. Harry, Miss Sadie. The answer is no, no, and no."

Zeke left the kitchen, and Sadie stared after him. "Well then, I guess he'll have to have Tenley's room."

"No, Miss Sadie!" Tallie cried. "Listen to me. That man is no good. Zeke brought his dirty uniform up for me to wash, and he said, 'that's not any officer's uniform.' He's right. There's no sergeant stripes on it, and I can't see where there ever has been. Don't you let him stay here."

"Perhaps he lost his original uniform while he was in the hospital," Sadie said.

"Oh, and perhaps General Scott slept in the tent with his men, too, and played cards with them."

"Just one night," Sadie said, setting two china cups on a tray.

"Rubbish." Tallie wagged her finger under Sadie's nose. "You just pinin' for Mr. Harry, and you all wrathy because he left so sudden. That's no reason to bring a shiftless stranger into the house."

"I'll take the coffee in. You see that his room is ready." Sadie picked up the tray.

"No. You can't do that." Tallie scurried around the worktable and tried to beat her to the door, but Sadie was too quick.

"I'm doing it," Sadie said.

"Then I have to sleep up here with you. Can't let no vagrant stay here with you unchaperoned."

"Fine." Already Sadie regretted her impulsiveness, but she was too stubborn to admit when she was wrong. Tallie's remark about Harry hit close to home. Her heart was aching, and this diversion had taken her mind off it. Well, she would send Mitchell away right after breakfast.

❧

Sadie woke and lay still for a moment. Moonlight shone in through her window, but it wasn't near dawn yet. She sat up and listened. Was that a step she'd heard? Too early for Tallie to be starting breakfast.

Another stealthy sound drew her attention. It sounded like the front door closing softly. She rose and tiptoed to the window, standing to the side and peering down into the yard.

It's nothing, she told herself. *Lord, calm my heart and let me rest.* She couldn't help but add, *And please let Harry forgive us, Lord! Give him peace, too.*

She still found it hard to believe Tallie's admission that she had continued the lie. She had told Mitchell that Papa was sick. How many tongue-lashings had she given Zeke for that very thing?

Sadie went back to bed and tossed fitfully, thinking about Harry and all the things they'd told him that couldn't be unsaid. At last her thoughts grew fuzzy with sleep.

fourteen

Harry left his garret room at the inn and went down the two flights of stairs to the dining room. Breakfast here was better than the dinner fare. He was served a high stack of flapjacks with sorghum, fried sausage, applesauce, and plenty of hot, strong coffee.

"You heading out today, Cooper?" the landlord asked when he pushed back his chair.

"I believe I will, sir."

The landlord nodded. "Good. I could rent your room three times over tonight."

"Something happening in town?" Harry asked.

"The traveling preacher pulled in yesterday. He's holding services today, and lots of folks will come in from the countryside."

Harry wondered if Sadie knew about this. If she did, she would probably come to Winchester to worship.

"Guess I lost track of the days," he said, trying to count them off mentally.

"It's Sunday all right," the landlord told him. "We take the parson whenever we can get him, though. Sometimes we have church on Friday or Tuesday. Folks stop their work and come."

Harry nodded. It was almost three months since he'd had the opportunity to attend a church service, and he felt a sudden longing to drink in God's Word. And this preacher knew the McEwan family. Harry might get a chance to talk to him. It wouldn't hurt him to stop over a day and let the dust settle between him and the McEwan farm.

"Where is the church service to be held?" he asked.

The landlord smiled. "At the schoolhouse."

"I think I'll stay until tomorrow, take a day of rest, and attend the service," Harry said.

The landlord's smile drooped. "As you wish. You're welcome."

"You won't lose money if I keep my room, will you?"

"Well, I suppose not. Not too much."

"What, you'd squeeze five or six people in that little closet?"

The landlord shrugged. "I might put a family with kids up there."

Harry thought that over for about a half second. "Well, I tell you what. If you can serve me breakfast again for supper tonight, I'll pay you extra."

"Oh, I don't know, sir. Mrs. Ferguson doesn't like to make special orders at dinnertime. It's too busy in the kitchen."

"Isn't it busy in the kitchen now?"

"Well, yes, sir, but the hired girls, Bessie and Emma, fix breakfast. My wife does lunch and dinner."

Harry reached into his pocket and produced a silver dollar. "Well, I'm paying for my room and tomorrow's breakfast in advance, and when I come back tonight there'd better not be any drunks or kids in my bed."

Mr. Ferguson nodded. "Yes, sir, and I'll tell Bessie you're partial to her flapjacks."

❧

When Sadie descended to the kitchen on Sunday morning, Tallie was preparing a breakfast tray.

"Is that for me?" Sadie asked. "I'm up."

"No." Tallie did not look up from her work but arranged the plate of bacon, eggs, and fried potatoes with painstaking care. "This is for your friend, Sergeant Mitchell. He can't come down for breakfast this mornin'. It's his leg, you know. It bothers him sometimes."

Sadie watched her with growing dismay. "Well, he was wounded in battle."

"Is that so? I never would have guessed it, but then I didn't have to. He's told me a hundred times in the last twelve hours." Tallie poured out a mug of tea for the tray.

Sadie wished she hadn't come downstairs. Tallie had lavished love on her since she was born, and Sadie knew she only wanted the best for her. Realizing she had been foolish in allowing Mitchell to stay overnight made it worse.

"He's making extra work for you, isn't he? Here, I'll take the tray up."

Tallie's back straightened, and she slapped at Sadie's hand. "Don't you touch that. You aren't going near that man's bedroom."

Sadie pulled away and twisted her hands together. "I'm sorry. You shouldn't have to wait on him."

"Not goin' to. I'll get Zeke to take the tray up as soon as he's in from the barn. Of course, the sergeant may object to his breakfast being served by a man who smells like the stable, but it'll be good for him to know that's part of life on a farm."

"He can't think we're rich, Tallie. This place is comfortable, but it's not like the grand places over near Richmond."

"I can't say what Sergeant Mitchell thinks, but I don't suppose it's anything good."

❧

Harry enjoyed the church service. He joined in with the others, singing hymns he had learned as a boy. Pastor Richards was of middle age, but robust and passionate. His sermon focused on God's holiness, and his message touched Harry's heart.

At the end of the service, the pastor announced that worship would reconvene at two o'clock. Folks brought lunches from their wagons and spread blankets on the grass in the schoolyard for a picnic.

Harry walked over to the boardinghouse for lunch then returned to the schoolyard. He spotted the pastor eating dessert with a family under the trees. When Pastor Richards rose and drifted toward another group, Harry walked over to him.

The pastor smiled and paused to talk to him, and Harry gave him a brief description of his background and the business that had brought him to the area.

"I've known Oliver McEwan for many years," Richards told Harry. "He's a fine man, and you can't do better than his horses. I was hoping to see him here today."

"Well, sir. . ." Harry stopped, wondering how much he should reveal. Since several families were within earshot, he decided it was not his place to break the news.

The pastor said with a frown, "Mr. McEwan wasn't well the last time I passed through. I hope he's not worse."

"Perhaps you could visit the family if you have time," Harry suggested.

"Yes, I think I can do that. He lost his son recently and was taking it quite hard when I saw him a month ago."

Harry nodded. "It would be a good thing for Miss Sadie if you could stop by and encourage her, I think. She's having some trouble handling her grief."

"I'll do it. Thank you, Mr. Cooper. It may be a day or two before I get out there, but I plan to stay with the Clarks until at least Wednesday. I'll be visiting folks in the area, and we'll hold another service Tuesday evening. I understand I've a wedding to perform, as well."

"They keep you busy when you come this way, sir?"

"Oh, indeed they do. My parish is large and scattered, Mr. Cooper, but I love serving the people."

The afternoon service gripped Harry's heart even more than the morning sermon had. When the pastor spoke of repentance and forgiveness, Harry at first thought about

Sadie, Zeke, and Tallie, and the lies they had told him. He prayed silently that they would seek God's forgiveness. But soon his thoughts turned inward, and he recognized his own anger and self-righteousness. He was not only in need of forgiveness; he had been unforgiving.

When the pastor closed the service, Harry slipped away and walked toward the river. He found a secluded spot beneath a large willow and dropped to his knees. *Lord, please take away all my selfishness and pride. Show me how to help Sadie.*

After a long time, he rose and headed back toward the inn. The sun was low over the mountains to the west, casting long shadows on the road. When he entered the dining room, Mr. Ferguson approached him with a smile.

"Glad to see you, Mr. Cooper. Bessie's husband let her come back after church to fix your supper. Or should I say breakfast?"

Harry grinned. "I'm obliged. If you don't mind, I'd like to meet Bessie."

"I guess she can spare half a minute. You want to wash up before you eat?"

Harry nodded.

"You wait here," Ferguson said.

A minute later a thin young woman came from the kitchen carrying a steaming pitcher.

"You Mr. Cooper?" she asked, approaching Harry.

He smiled at her. Her huge apron enveloped her like a shroud. She must have borrowed one from Mrs. Ferguson. "Thank you for coming back to work just for me. I didn't mean to take you away from your family on the Lord's Day."

Bessie smiled as she held out the pitcher of water. "My Joe says I make the best flapjacks in Virginia. To hear him tell it, that's why he married me."

Harry chuckled and reached into his pocket. "Is Mr. Ferguson paying you extra?"

"My regular wage, sir, but don't you worry none."

Harry slipped a coin into her hand. "That's for you, not the boss."

Her eyes widened. "You don't need to pay for your supper twice, sir."

"Consider it a tax on my selfishness. Reverend Richards and the Lord have been working on me this afternoon." Harry took the pitcher from her.

Bessie's warm smile rewarded him. "Thank you, sir. Wasn't the service wonderful? Your plate will be ready in five minutes."

Harry went up the stairs as quickly as he could without spilling the water. Again he wished he was dining at the McEwan table tonight, and Tallie's cooking was only a small part of his longing.

Lord, take care of Sadie tonight. Ease her sorrow, and please, if You don't mind, I'm asking You to prepare her to let me take care of her.

❧

Tallie trudged up the stairs with an early supper tray. Might as well feed the voracious visitor before the others came in for their supper. All this stair climbing was wearing her out. She missed Sadie's help in the kitchen this evening, but Zeke had gotten behind in the barn chores. Even though it was Sunday, Sadie had put on her old gray dress and gone down to help him and Pax tend the horses.

Tallie didn't like it one bit when her mistress worked like a field hand. Maybe they should send Pax to his brother's house in the morning. If Ephraim could give them a few days' work now, it would be a big help. Of course, they needed to straighten out this business of Mr. Oliver's death before too many people came around. If only Sergeant Mitchell would leave!

She reached the landing and paused for breath before

heading for Tenley's old bedroom. They had put just the barest of furnishings back in there as the wall repairs were not completed. *Besides,* she thought, *no sense making the stranger too comfortable.*

The door was open, and she stopped just outside it. "Mr. Mitchell? Got your supper here."

There was no response, and she cautiously peeked around the doorjamb. The bed was empty.

Tallie's heart skipped a beat. She walked into the bedroom and took a good look around to be sure. She set the tray on the stand next to the bed. He must have decided to make a trip out back to the necessary, but if so, she ought to have heard him go down the stairs.

She hurried back into the hallway. As she reached the top of the stairs a muffled sound reached her, and she froze. Someone was in Mr. Oliver's bedroom.

fifteen

"What are you doin' in here?"

Mitchell quickly shut the top dresser drawer and faced her. He was fully clothed, and he looked fit to her.

"Well now, it's Tallie, the efficient cook-housemaid. I was just looking for some company. Got lonesome down at the other end of the house and thought maybe Mr. McEwan was as bored as I was. Thought we could have a game of checkers maybe. But it seems Mr. McEwan stepped out." His feral smile made Tallie shiver.

"You nothin' but trouble. You git out of here!" She stepped aside, indicating that he should avail himself of the open door.

"Here now, is that any way to talk to your master's guest?"

"What do you know about it?"

"I know plenty. I know no one's living in this room. Somebody's been sorting through Mr. McEwan's things." Mitchell nodded toward the bed where Tallie had spread out piles of clothing she removed from the wardrobe, hoping Sadie would go through them tomorrow. He ran a finger along the edge of the dresser and looked at it critically. "Dust, too. For shame, Tallie. You haven't been doing your job. Letting the patient's room get all dusty. I've been listening, too. No one took Mr. McEwan a tray all day. I thought the poor man was starving, but now I see it's worse than that."

Tallie shifted her weight, making herself stare back at him. "You don't know what you're talkin' about. Now go on out of here."

He smiled and walked past her into the hallway. Tallie leaned against the door and took a deep breath. She looked about the room, wondering if he had stolen any of Mr. Oliver's things. She couldn't tell without making a careful examination. *I'll come up after dinner,* she decided. She closed the door.

Mitchell had stopped in the hallway near the top of the stairs. Tallie heard Sadie's surprised voice.

"Why, Sergeant Mitchell, you're up and about. That's good news. Your leg must be better."

"Yes, ma'am, it is," he said smoothly. "I was just casting about for some company."

Tallie strode up to stand near Mitchell. "He been snoopin' in your father's room, Miss Sadie."

A look of fear crossed Sadie's face. "What—" She stared at Mitchell.

Tallie said, "I was gonna tell him Mr. Oliver is gone, but he got no manners."

Mitchell smiled. "Oh, he's gone, all right."

Sadie swallowed hard. "If your leg is so much better, Sergeant Mitchell, I expect you are able to leave us."

"Well, miss, it's a trifle better, but I wouldn't want to try to walk five miles into town on it tonight."

Sadie hesitated, and Tallie tried to think of a solution. *Don't give in,* she thought, and she tried to send semaphore to that effect in Sadie's direction with her eyes.

"Fine," Sadie said. "Our man, Zeke, can drive you to Winchester in the morning."

"I'd be grateful, miss. And I do regret not being able to see your father. My condolences. I'll see you at dinner." He turned toward his room.

"I done put your supper tray by your bed," Tallie called.

He smiled at her then looked at Sadie. "That's very kind, but I feel well enough to get to the dining room this evening."

Tallie scowled at Sadie, but Sadie merely said, "Then I shall see you in thirty minutes, sir."

❧

Tallie followed Sadie to the door of her room.

"Please, Tallie, I need a few minutes alone."

"I was just goin' to help you get changed, Miss Sadie."

"Send Pax up with some hot water. I can do for myself. When I'm dressed, I'll come down to the kitchen, and we can discuss this."

"Yes'm." Tallie faded back behind her, and Sadie entered the sanctuary of her bedroom. Had Mitchell sneaked in here, as well? Had he looked at her personal things, handled her clothing, books, and stationery? She looked around carefully and decided he had not. Not a thing was out of place, so far as she could tell. She had left a silver dollar and two nickels in plain view on her secretary, along with a silver pen and some stamps. If Mitchell had been in here and his purposes were as nefarious as Tallie and Zeke indicated, he surely would have pilfered the coins.

Pax knocked at the door and delivered her hot water. Sadie hastily washed and changed into her blue dress. She brushed her hair smooth and took a moment before the mirror to check her appearance. How she wished Harry were here, preparing to meet her for dinner! How could she have been so foolish as to deceive him and drive him away? If he'd been present when Mitchell arrived, no doubt he'd have run him off immediately.

She wished she didn't have to face the sergeant over the dinner table. He made her nervous, and apparently he saw through Tallie's attempt to continue the fiction that her father was alive. Mitchell wasn't a large man, but he seemed fit and agile. She doubted he would attempt to harm any of them physically, but his implications put her on edge. He had made himself charming last night. She hoped he would again be on his best behavior tonight. At any rate, she'd be glad when he was out of the house.

When she entered the kitchen, Zeke and Pax were seated at the table eating their supper. Sadie knew Pax would start washing the dishes afterward while Zeke and Tallie waited on her and Mitchell. It was the dinnertime routine of the household.

"I wish he was gone," she blurted. "I wish I was eating in here with you all tonight!"

"There now," Tallie said. "He be leavin' in the mornin'. Then we'll get back to rights."

Pax stared at her. "You look fine, Miss Sadie, but your face is as white as Mama's apron."

"Thank you, Pax. It gave me a start to see Sergeant Mitchell looking so. . .healthy."

"Healthy and active," Tallie said as she lifted the fried chicken pieces onto a platter. "He was making free of the house, and that ain't right. I don't believe his leg was botherin' him. In fact—" She shook her long-handled fork at Sadie. "In fact, I don't believe he ever was wounded. He made that up for sympathy and for an excuse to stay longer."

Sadie grimaced, ruing her gullibility. "He does look spry this evening."

"That's right," said Tallie. "This mornin' he claimed he couldn't get down the stairs 'cause he hurt so bad, but now he's right as a trivet."

"It must have been all the exercise he put in last night that made him sore," Zeke said, sipping his tea.

Sadie frowned at him. "What do you mean?"

"Nothin' except the little stroll your guest took last night—or should I say this mornin'? It was past midnight, after all."

Sadie remembered her restlessness in the night and wondered if Mitchell's movements had wakened her. She stared at Zeke, but he wouldn't look back, so she walked over to the table and stood directly across from him. Pax looked up at her in surprise.

"If you know something I should know, Zeke, you'd best tell me now." Sadie tapped her foot impatiently.

Zeke wiped his mouth with his sleeve and finally met her gaze. "I don't know nothin', Miss Sadie. I just saw your friend leave the house last night, and it didn't look to me like his leg was botherin' him then, not one little bit. He wasn't favorin' it in the least."

"Where did he go?"

Zeke shrugged. "He started down the lane then took off into the woods. Your guess is as good as mine."

Sadie took three deep, controlled breaths.

"I've asked him to leave in the morning. As a matter of fact, Zeke, I told him you'd drive him to town."

"I'll do what you say, Miss Sadie, but I don't think that tramp is helpless. He takes on about his leg painin' him so, and that makes folks cater to him." Zeke lifted his teacup.

"Should I march upstairs and demand that he vacate the premises immediately?"

"Do it!" Tallie cried.

Zeke shook his head. "Let's not give him any reason to be huffy with us. You've been nothin' but gracious, Miss Sadie. If I take him to town in the mornin', we'll be sure he gets there, and he can't say we weren't polite to him."

Sadie nodded slowly. "All right then. First thing after breakfast."

❧

Mitchell poured on the charm at dinner, but Sadie wasn't receptive this time. When he hinted that she might hire him to help with the farm work, since she seemed a little short on manpower these days, she bristled.

"Excuse me, Sergeant. I'm very fatigued. Zeke will bring you coffee."

Mitchell jumped up as she rose. "Wait! Aren't we going to sit in the parlor? I thought I'd tell you more about Tenley.

Maybe you'd like to hear about how we marched across the desert for weeks, chasing Santa Anna."

Sadie shook her head. "I believe I've heard enough. I hope you'll have a good journey in the morning. Zeke is having an early breakfast and leaving for town immediately afterward. Good-bye, Sergeant Mitchell."

She swept around, hoops and all, and glided through the door and up the stairs. When she reached her room she closed the door behind her and exhaled. She hoped Tallie would come up soon to unlace her corset. She ought to go and help with the kitchen work, but it seemed beyond her strength tonight. She wanted to be alone and safe in her room. She didn't have her father, and she didn't have Harry, but she had God with her always, and she would enjoy His company tonight.

She untied the waist of her crinoline and dropped the awkward skirt hoops, stepped out over them and sat down in her rocker. She sat deep in thought for several minutes then reached for her Bible. Only one person could show her what best to do now, and she would listen to Him.

A half hour later she heard Mitchell's heavy, uneven steps on the stairs. It was nearly as long again before Tallie came to help her undress, and Sadie noted how slow her steps were.

"You're working too hard, Tallie."

"Just doin' my job."

"No, you're doing the work of three people. I should have stayed downstairs to help you with the kitchen work."

"I'll be fine as soon as we get that baggage out of your brother's room. But you can help me make jelly tomorrow. Pax tells me the grapes are just right."

Sadie smiled. "I'll do that."

Tallie untied the corset laces, and Sadie shrugged out of it and into her warm flannel nightgown. "You could sleep in Papa's room now," Sadie said.

"You afraid to be up here alone with him?"

"No, it's not that. I just thought you might be more comfortable than in that little cot you have in the pantry."

Tallie sighed. "If the truth be told, I'd be more comfortable in my own bed, but I couldn't never sleep in the master's room. But I don't like you bein' up here with him."

"We could put a cot here in my room for you," Sadie suggested.

Tallie frowned. "Not tonight, we can't. Zeke's gone down to the cabin. You just lock your door tight, you hear me?"

"I will."

Tallie sighed. "What we gonna do, Miss Sadie? After he's gone, I mean. We can't have you rattlin' around in this house alone every night, but Zeke won't put up with this arrangement forever."

"I don't know. I did think perhaps Ephraim and Dulcy might come stay here and help us."

"Eph won't want to give up his blacksmithin' business."

"I know. Maybe we could let him build a cabin here. They're renting where they live now. If they'd live on McEwan land, I'd give him free rent just for the security, and his smithing customers could come here. It's only a few miles from where he is now, and folks will travel a long ways for a good blacksmith."

"Maybe," Tallie said with a yawn. "But Dulcy wouldn't be sleepin' here in the big house, and you know you can't afford to pay much extra help right now."

Sadie frowned and sat down on the edge of her bed. "We need to clear things up about the title to the land. If I can own the farm outright, we can make a go of it, Tallie. I know we can, even if we have to hire more help. Zeke is smart when it comes to horses. I know Papa wasn't too happy with Clipper's prospects, but there's that yearling colt, the one Papa called Smidge. Harry was impressed with his conformation. If Smidge turns out as well as we think he might, I'd have the stallion we need, and we could expand our breeding operation in a couple of years."

"Hush now," said Tallie. "It's not proper for you to talk about those things. You ought not to say *stallion*."

Sadie giggled. "All right then, *gentleman horse*."

There was a moment's silence as Tallie began to brush her mistress's hair. Her touch was gentle, and Sadie felt the tension drain out of her.

"Mr. Harry knows about things like that," Tallie said. "Maybe if he comes back, you can have Zeke ask him for some advice."

Sadie felt a lump in her throat. "I don't think he's coming back, Tallie. He's had all day yesterday and today. He's probably halfway to Kentucky by now."

"He left those mares."

Sadie turned and looked up at Tallie. "What if he never comes back? Even worse, what if he writes and asks for his money? You know I can't pay it back."

Tallie was silent for a moment. "You been prayin', child?"

Sadie was humbled by her simple question. "Yes. When I pray I get to thinking everything will turn out all right, but afterward I forget, and I get to worrying again. Tallie, I can't count on Harry's goodness. Men fail you. Even the Bible says so. And I failed him so badly, I don't blame him."

"Yes, men do fail you on occasion, but the Bible also tells you not to fret."

Sadie inhaled slowly. "Tallie, will you pray with me now?" She grasped her cook's hand and pulled her down on the quilt beside her. They murmured their petitions quietly. Tears rolled freely down Sadie's face as she prayed.

"And help me to trust You more and to quit worrying so about Harry and the property and everything, Father. In Jesus' name—" She heard a thud, seemingly from below them. "Amen," she said quickly. "Did you hear that, Tallie?"

"I heard it. My menfolk left the house a half an hour ago."

They both stood up. Sadie fumbled for her dressing gown.

"You can't go downstairs like that," Tallie chided.

Sadie hesitated then grabbed her gray housedress. "We could be robbed blind in the time it takes to do all these buttons," she muttered.

"Let me take a quick look. It's probably just Zeke checkin' on things." Tallie lit a candle from the flame of the oil lamp and headed for the door.

"I'm coming, too." Sadie grabbed the poker that hung beside the hearth. She rarely had a fire in her bedroom fireplace, but the small poker Tallie's son Ephraim had made for her seemed the perfect size for a defensive weapon.

"Watch out," Tallie hissed. "You gonna get soot all over your clothes."

"Well, Zeke took Papa's pistol down to the kitchen yesterday. We don't have anything else."

Tallie said no more but tiptoed into the hall carrying the candle.

When they reached the top of the stairs she stopped, and Sadie pushed in beside her, staring downward. Light came from the parlor doorway, and they could hear low voices. Tallie blew out her candle, and they stood listening.

"No, don't bother with that," Mitchell said distinctly. Another male voice answered, but Sadie couldn't make out what he said.

Sadie started down the stairs.

"Come back here!" Tallie whispered. "Where you goin'?"

Sadie stopped with one hand on the balustrade, looking up at her. "I'm not going to stand by and let my home be ransacked under my nose."

"You ain't even fully dressed, child."

Sadie gave a soundless laugh. "I have to wear a corset to confront a thief?"

She hurried down the steps and to the door of the parlor. The small oil lamp was burning on her father's desk, illuminating Dan Mitchell and another man. Mitchell was wearing the clothes she had given him, and the other man was dressed much as the sergeant had been on his arrival. He was larger, and the side of his face was scarred. In one hand he held a bulging cotton pillowcase, one Sadie recognized as having been on Mitchell's bed. Many years ago her mother had embroidered it with magnolias. The idea of the filthy robber carrying off her mother's delicate work enraged Sadie.

"You want these doodads?" the man nodded toward the porcelain figurines on the mantelpiece.

"Yes, but be careful not to break them," Mitchell said. "Those knickknacks can be valuable. There's a lot of stuff upstairs. I got what cash I could find before I was interrupted, but I saw a rifle and a store of lead balls in the old man's room and a couple of knives, besides a pocket watch and a fine painting. I expect the girl has jewelry, too."

"We'll get those after," the second man said.

"You'll do no such thing." Sadie stepped into the room.

sixteen

Mitchell whirled, and both men stared at her.

"Well, now, if it isn't the lady of the house," Mitchell said, smiling as he stepped toward her.

"Stay back." Sadie brandished the poker and held her ground. Her heart raced as she met the sergeant's malevolent glare.

Mitchell laughed. "My, oh, my, we are fierce."

"You didn't tell me she was a firebrand," the big man said. One step and he was so close that, before Sadie could swing the poker, he had it in his hands and twisted it, wrenching it away from her. He tossed it to Mitchell and jerked Sadie around so that her back was to him, and she felt something sharp at her throat.

"All right, Miss McEwan." Mitchell smiled and paced before her as the larger man held her. "Moe doesn't want to hurt you. Just tell us where the family fortune lies, and we'll be gone."

Sadie stared at him, too terrified to squeak. *Family fortune,* she thought. *Either Tenley painted a very rosy picture of our life to this fellow, or he's gotten the impression somewhere else.* It was true her father had a large piece of land with prime river frontage. The house was adequate, but not opulent. The horses were the finest, but that was because her father had spent many years working hard to build up his breeding stock.

The man holding her squeezed her until she could barely breathe. "Where's the money?" he croaked in her ear.

Sadie struggled to turn her head away. The stench of his breath was sickening, and his body odor made her feel ill. She hated the way he held her so tightly.

"Let me go," she whispered. "I don't have any money."

Mitchell laughed. "I heard the slave boy say you sold several horses a week or so ago. Where's the cash? There's got to be more than we've found lying around."

Sadie held perfectly still, trying not to visualize the carved pine jewel box on her dresser. In it lay the money she had left after buying the lumber and new windows. She had hoped to purchase winter supplies with it. Of course, they would find it sooner or later.

"Where is it?" Moe snarled in her ear.

Sadie gulped for air and managed to gasp, "He's not a slave."

"Oh, that's right. Your brother told me his grandpa was a soft touch and freed them all." Mitchell came close and leaned toward her. "He also told me your old man was well fixed. The sooner you tell us, the sooner we'll be gone."

"Tenley wouldn't—" Sadie broke off as Mitchell raised his hand.

He's going to strike me! She tried to pull back, but that meant leaning closer to Moe. She sobbed at her own helplessness and fear.

"Hold it, mister!"

Both men turned in surprise to the doorway. Tallie stood there in suppressed fury, and in her hands was Oliver's old pistol.

There was an instant of silence; then Mitchell laughed.

"Tallie, Tallie, Tallie. Don't expect me to believe that thing is loaded." He started to step toward her, and the pistol fired with a deafening roar that made Sadie's ears ring. One of the new windowpanes shattered. They all stood staring at Tallie; then Mitchell smiled.

"Well done, Tallie. Now we know how serious you are about protecting your mistress. We also know the chamber is empty now. Give me that thing." He stepped forward and took the gun from Tallie's nerveless hand. "These old pistols." He shook his head as he examined it. "Single shot. Not much good once you've fired it."

Sadie caught Tallie's eye, hoping to see some reassurance there. Had she awakened Zeke and Pax, or had she only had time to go to the kitchen for the pistol? Tallie's eyes were dull with despair. Sadie refused to let herself give up hope. Maybe Zeke had heard the gun's report.

"What are you going to do with us?" she asked.

Mitchell looked up. "You got more ammo for this?"

Sadie and Tallie kept quiet, and he laughed. "Right. You know, Moe and I aren't murderers, which is more than I can say for you, Tallie. You'd have blown my head off with glee if you could've held your hands steady."

Moe let out a guffaw, and Sadie renewed her struggle. His grip tightened, and she hated having his hands on her.

"Easy now," Mitchell said. He gestured toward the door. "Ladies, upstairs, please."

"You want them in the heiress's bedroom?" Moe asked, allowing Sadie to precede him into the hallway.

"No, put them in the room where I've been staying." Mitchell came behind them, carrying the lamp. "We know there's nothing worthwhile in there. It will keep them out of our way while we finish our work."

Sadie thought of making a break for the front door, but Moe placed his hulk of a body between her and freedom. He cut the air before him with his knife and said, "Go on now. Get up those stairs."

Sadie and Tallie went up in silence. Mitchell herded them into his bedchamber and took a quick look around. "I think they'll be secure here, Moe, but let's be quick."

He took the key from the inside of the keyhole, and the two men went out. It was dark when they closed the door.

Sadie heard the click of the key in the lock. Her knees went weak all of a sudden, and she felt for the edge of the bed and sank down on it.

"Tallie, we'd best pray."

"That's right," Tallie said, walking to the window. "But we'd best be thinkin' while we pray."

"Do you think Zeke will help us?"

"Can't count on it. If he was still up, he'd hear that pistol shot for certain. If not. . .well, when that man is out, he's out."

Sadie nodded in misery. "He said he didn't sleep well last night so he was tired tonight. He's probably down there in the cabin, snoring away."

"Sawin' logs," Tallie agreed. "So it's up to us."

Sadie joined her at the window. "Too bad they finished the outside work and took the ladder down."

Tallie grunted. "I be too wide to get through this window anyway. I'd bust the nice frame Mr. Harry made. But you now. . ." She turned to Sadie. "You can get out the window. I'll help you."

Alarm shot through Sadie as she eyed the window casement. "But there's no ladder."

"Bedsheets. Good, sturdy, linen bedsheets. Come on. We'll tie them together. Hurry up. Those men won't stick around long, and we want to put Zeke onto them before they get away with everythin' you own."

"Do you think Zeke can stop them any more than we did? I don't want anyone to get hurt."

"I don't know if he can or not, but my man has a strange habit of thinkin' when he needs to. Sometimes you'd guess he didn't have a brain in his head, but when he wants, he can be smart as a steel trap."

Sadie sobbed as she yanked the comforter off the bed. "Tallie, I left all the money Harry gave me in my jewel box. They've probably found it by now."

"Well, we can't help that." Tallie knotted two corners of the sheets together. "You think this will be long enough, or should we tear them in two?"

"Don't do that! Linen sheets don't grow on trees, you know. I can jump the last bit, if I need to."

"All right, but you be careful! Remember all the glass that was under the ladder? I think Zeke got most of it, but they might be a few pieces left."

Sadie stared at the window. "I can't go out that one, Tallie. It's right above the front parlor window. Those hooligans might see me." She went to the second window, on the sidewall of the house.

"That one's above a parlor window, too," Tallie said.

"Not directly, and besides it's not where the broken glass was." Sadie raised the sash.

Tallie brought the one chair over and planted it beneath the window. Sadie climbed onto it and stuck her feet out, clinging to the sheets.

"You hang on tight," Sadie said.

"I will," Tallie assured her. "It's too short to tie around the bedstead. Maybe we ought to rip them, after all."

"No! Besides we don't have anything to cut them with, and they're too stout to tear with our bare hands."

Before Tallie could say anymore, Sadie lowered herself from the window frame. She dangled above the earth for a second, wondering if she could survive this escapade. She knew she didn't have the strength to pull herself back up to the windowsill, so there was only one way to go. She inched downward as slowly as she could, hoping to touch the ground soon with her toes.

She heard Tallie moan, and Sadie called softly, "You all right?"

"Hurry up, gal. I'm no great shakes as a hitchin' post."

Sadie almost lost her grip when she reached the knot at

the bottom of the first sheet. The bulk of the second sheet seemed too thick for her hands to grip firmly. She realized her legs were close to the side parlor window. What if the men were in there and saw her or heard her feet bump the wall? The sheets billowed out in a sudden breeze, and she slipped unceremoniously the last four feet, landing in a heap between the side of the house and a rosebush.

She held her breath. No sound came from within the house, and the parlor window was dark. They must not have returned to the room.

Probably tearing my bedroom to pieces, she thought bitterly.

"You alive?" Tallie called in a stage whisper.

"Yes. Now hush. I'll get us some help."

Sadie stood up and edged past the prickly rosebush, shaking out her dress. She lifted her skirt and prepared to dash around the corner and across the yard toward Zeke's cabin. She rounded the corner at a full run and slammed into something firm but yielding.

"Oof!"

Sadie and the man she had collided with tumbled to the ground.

seventeen

"Hold it!" Zeke yelled.

Sadie wanted to laugh, but she couldn't catch her breath.

"It's me, Zeke," she gasped.

"Miss Sadie?" He clutched her arm then fumbled in the dimness, roughly patting her head. "Well, sure enough. Where'd you come from?"

"I dropped from the sky."

Zeke shook his head and pulled himself to his feet then offered her his strong hand. "I thought I heard a gunshot."

"You did. Tallie fired my father's pistol at Mitchell and his thieving pal, but unfortunately she missed them both."

"Do tell!" Zeke peered at her in the little light offered by the thin crescent moon. "Where are they now?"

"Probably stealing the cash Harry gave us out of my jewel box. They're taking everything they can lay their hands on, Zeke! And the big fellow, Moe, has a knife." She brushed at her skirt.

"Are you all right? Where's Tallie?"

"I'm fine. She's up in Tenley's room. They locked us in there a few minutes ago, and Tallie let me out the window. I climbed down the bedsheets."

Zeke laughed. "Well, well. Ain't you some punkins?"

"It's not funny, Zeke. What can we do? They're robbing us blind, and the big man doesn't care if he knocks a few heads together."

Suddenly she heard hoofbeats, and she stared toward the barnyard. "What's that?"

"Don't worry, Miss Sadie. I woke Pax when I heard the shot

and told him to get over to the barn and saddle Clipper and ride for town. There's no horse faster than Clipper in these parts."

"That was good thinking, if Pax can handle him."

Zeke smiled. "He'll do, and he's got the moonlight to guide him, praise the Lawd. I figured whatever was up, we'd need some help. Maybe I should have sent him to Kauffmans'. It's closer, but the road is poor goin' that way, and I figure there's a chance Pax will find Mr. Harry at the inn."

Sadie caught her breath. "Do you really think so? I expect he's long gone."

"Well, then, I allow Pax can raise the alarm in town."

Relief swept over Sadie. "I'm so glad I found you! I was frightened for a while, I don't mind telling you."

Zeke pulled her up against the side of the house. Sadie followed his gaze and saw that a light had appeared in the parlor window. She held her breath.

Zeke edged toward the glass and peered into the room then ducked down beside her. "They's goin' through Mr. Oliver's desk."

"Oh, Zeke, there's no time!" she whispered. "They'll be out of here long before Pax gets back with help."

"Listen now. They're collectin' a lot of booty."

"Yes, I saw them with a pillowcase full earlier, and that was just from the parlor."

Zeke stroked his chin. "They've got your papa's rifle now and a pile of other stuff. So I asks you, Miss Sadie, how's they going to carry all that stuff away from here?"

She drew in a quick breath. "The horses! They're going to steal some horses and maybe the buggy or the farm wagon."

"That's right. For a quick getaway, I'm bankin' on two horses."

"What can we do?"

"Come on!"

He grabbed her hand and pulled her toward the barn.

When they reached the door he opened it quietly. Several horses whinnied and shifted in their stalls.

"Here now. Can you lead that first mare out in the dark without gettin' stepped on? I don't think we'd ought to light the lantern."

"I can do it," Sadie said.

"Good. We'll put them all out to pasture. That will at least slow them crooks down some."

Sadie reached up and gave him a swift hug. "Thank you, Zeke. It's a good thing they didn't hear Pax leave."

"Godspeed that boy. Now you get the mares one at a time. We'll get Mr. Harry's mares out first. Don't want them stolen. Then your mares and the colts. I'll see to Star last, and if there's time we'll hide all the bridles in the hayloft."

They ran back and forth, releasing the horses into the pasture. Sadie led one mare on each trip, but Zeke was able to control two horses at a time, and the barn emptied swiftly. Sadie puffed at the exertion and was grateful she wasn't wearing the despised corset.

We're going to make it, she thought as she released Lily's five-month-old filly into the fenced field. She wished Tallie could know what they were doing, but there was no time to get word to her now. Sadie hoped her dear servant would take her own advice and not fret.

She bounded along the path toward the barn door. Zeke had gone in to get Star, the last horse. While he took the aging stallion to the pasture, she would conceal the bridles.

A glow of light caught her eye, and she stopped in dismay twenty yards from the barn. Dan Mitchell and his friend had come down from the house and had nearly reached the barn door. They each lugged a sack of plunder, and Moe was carrying her father's rifle.

Sadie sank into the shadows at the edge of the barn and sent up a quick prayer for guidance. The two men lowered their pillowcases full of loot to the ground outside the door then went inside. She listened intently but didn't hear anything. Her heart raced as she crept forward. Feeling her way gingerly, she took hold of the first pillowcase and dragged it toward the watering trough then got the second bundle. She didn't take the time to remove them farther, but the dark shadows concealed them.

She tiptoed to the doorway and leaned her head past the edge to look inside. Mitchell and Moe had their backs to her. Mitchell was holding the lantern high while Moe aimed the rifle at Zeke.

Zeke stared at the men in the glare of the lantern. His eyes flickered from one to the other, and for an instant Sadie thought he focused on her then looked back at Moe. He held the lead rope with his left hand, and his right was grasping Star's halter with a firm grip. The horse fidgeted and snorted then pawed the earthen floor impatiently.

"Well now, Sergeant Mitchell," Zeke said. "Were you aimin' to take a ride this evening? It's a might late."

"What are you doing out here in the dark, Zeke?" Mitchell asked.

"Just tendin' this here horse, suh. He was makin' a ruckus, and I thought I'd put him out in the paddock, or he'd never let me get any sleep."

Mitchell looked around at the empty stalls. "Where are the other horses?"

"They all out to pasture for the night, suh. We let them stay out to graze sometimes when the weather's good."

"Step away from the horse," Moe said.

"Oh, no, suh, I couldn't do that. If I let go of his halter, they's no tellin' what this horse will do."

Sadie gulped down the fear that rose in her chest. She had the feeling that if Zeke did as told, Moe would shoot him as soon as he was clear of the horse.

Lord, show me how I can help Zeke! She wondered where the pitchfork was, but it was probably down at the other end of the barn, beyond Zeke, where they usually stored it, along with the other tools and all the harness. She crept through the doorway and flattened herself against the wall.

"Oh, that horse is a brute, is he?" Mitchell asked.

"I'll take him," Moe said with a laugh.

Mitchell nodded at Zeke. "Tie him up and throw a saddle on him."

"Oh, suh, don't make me do that. This here's Mr. Oliver's special horse, and he never lets anyone else ride him."

"Shut up! You fool, you think I don't know the truth? Your master's dead, and you've been helping the girl keep it quiet so you can go on living here. Got yourself a pretty soft place so long as no one knows about it, don't you?"

Zeke's eyes were wide with fright. "That's not so, suh."

Mitchell smiled. "The way I see it, her brother was the heir, and now he's dead. Sadie McEwan is paying you and your wife to help her out, and you're giving her a facade of respectability. If no one finds out she's alone, she can go on living as she's accustomed, until she snares a husband."

Moe shook his head dolefully. "Too bad she didn't like you, Dan. Think she'd like me? Maybe we should stay."

Mitchell scowled. "No. If we did, Miss McEwan would have the law on us before sunset tomorrow. Time to move along, Moe."

Zeke's eyes narrowed. "If we're gonna talk plain, mistuh, you'd best think twice before you rob the McEwan family blind."

"Oh, you're going to stop me?"

"I might."

"You'll do what I tell you," Mitchell snarled. "Now saddle that horse and fetch me one from the pasture. A fast one, you hear?"

"I told you, suh—this horse ain't the one you want to take for a pleasure ride."

Sadie knew Zeke was trying to buy time, but she couldn't think what to do that would help him. In an alcove near the door was a barrel of oats, and on a ledge in the barn wall were several brushes, a tin of salve, and a used horseshoe with several bent nails still dangling from its holes.

She eased cautiously toward the wall and grasped the horseshoe. She remembered playing a game with Tenley once where they'd tried to throw the horseshoes Ephraim pulled off the carriage horses' feet into a bucket. She hadn't been very good at it.

❧

"Mr. Harry! Mr. Harry! Wake up!"

Harry sat bolt upright in bed. Someone was pounding on the door. In an instant he remembered he was in the attic of the inn in Winchester, Virginia. His next conscious thought was that Pax was screaming for him to open the door.

"Mr. Harry!"

"I'm coming!" He grabbed his pants and pulled them on hastily then dashed to unlock the door.

Pax fell into the room, and Harry caught him.

"Easy now. No sense busting your noggin. What's the matter?"

"The soldier," Pax panted.

"Soldier? What soldier?"

"The one called Mitchell. He's doing somethin' bad. My pa heard a gunshot from the house where this soldier is. He sent me to get you. You gotta come, Mr. Harry. We don't know what he's doing to my mama and Miss Sadie."

Harry stared at him.

"You telling it straight? Who is this fellow?"

"We don't know, suh. He showed up yestiddy, out of nowhere, saying he was a friend of Mr. Tenley."

Harry threw his shirt on as he talked and sat down to poke his feet in his boots.

"I'll have to get Pepper from the stable, out back of the inn."

"No, suh, I done brought Clipper. You take him, and I'll come along on Pepper. Iffen you don't mind, suh."

"Good plan!" Harry grabbed his hat and wallet and tore down the stairs. He heard Pax behind him, and at the bottom of the second flight of steps, he turned for a moment.

"Get Mr. Ferguson. Tell him to raise some other men and come out to the farm."

"Yes, suh."

"Good lad." Harry ran outside and found the four-year-old stallion fighting the rope that held him fast to the hitching rail in front of the inn. He untied the rope and gathered the reins. Clipper snuffled and stepped away from him. Harry remembered Zeke cautioning him once that Clipper didn't like to stand still to be mounted. He didn't like to be switched back of the saddle either, if Harry recalled it right. He took a few precious seconds to calm the stallion and push him up against the edge of the porch then jumped quickly onto his back. Clipper leaped toward the street, and Harry let him tear for home.

❧

"Here, take this." Mitchell thrust the lantern toward his partner. Moe took it and reluctantly surrendered the rifle to him. Mitchell stepped closer to Zeke. "All right now, saddle that horse, or I'll blow your head off."

"Yes, suh." Zeke meekly turned Star toward the back wall of the barn. Sadie knew an iron ring was in a post there. One was closer to the barn door, right beside where she was standing. Zeke was taking Star as far away from the door and her as possible, to delay the thieves' discovering her presence. As the two ruffians watched Zeke and Star move away from them, Sadie figured it was now or never.

She swung her arm back and put all her strength into the toss, aiming for the back of Mitchell's head.

To her horror she saw the horseshoe fly over Mitchell's shoulder and beyond him. He and Moe both jumped and stared as the shoe hit Star squarely on the hindquarters.

The stallion screamed in terror and reared, jerking his head away from Zeke. Zeke lost his grip on the halter, and Star pivoted on his hind feet then lunged toward the barn door with Zeke doing his best to hang on to the lead rope. The horse ran between Mitchell and his friend. Mitchell was jostled so that he stepped backward, flinging the gun upward, but Star's shoulder slammed into Moe. The big man lost his balance and fell backward to the floor.

"Run!" Zeke yelled to Sadie, struggling to hold Star back by the rope, but as Moe's lantern struck the floor the bedding straw of the nearest stall burst into flames, and Sadie shrank into the corner by the oat barrel. Star squealed and turned again, kicking as he wrenched the rope away from Zeke. The horse bolted to the back of the barn once more and stood trembling and pawing the ground.

"Miss Sadie!" Zeke grabbed her wrist. "Quick now! Get out of here!"

"No, Zeke! The barn!"

"We can't stop it," he cried. The flames were already engulfing the dry wood of the stall dividers. She knew it might only be seconds before the hayloft above them erupted into a crackling inferno.

"We can't leave Star!" She clung to Zeke's hand.

Mitchell dashed through the burning straw on the barn floor and past them toward the open door. Sadie choked as the roiling smoke reached her. The stallion's shriek came to her from beyond the spreading fire.

eighteen

Harry galloped up the lane to the McEwans' house, praying he would be in time to help. The house was dark, but he saw movement at an upper window, the one he and Zeke had dropped the frame from. A stout figure leaned from the window. The face was dark above a snowy white garment.

"The barn!"

"Tallie?" he called.

"The barn, Mr. Harry! Hurry!"

Clipper was already fighting him to return to the barn, and Harry let him have his head. As they sped closer to the large structure, he saw the flicker of flames through the doorway, and a wave of smoke hit him.

Clipper whinnied and reared. As Harry tried to control the stallion, a man came running out the barn door. Harry didn't stop to think, beyond the certainty that the pale-faced man was not Zeke, and leaped from the saddle onto the fleeing figure.

He carried the man to the ground with him, and they rolled in the dust of the barnyard, wrestling for control. Harry concentrated on subduing his adversary, but he was also conscious of Clipper snorting and dancing about them and a second man yelling.

It was only seconds, but it seemed forever before he pinioned the man on the ground. In a glance he saw a huge man pulling Clipper's head around toward his shoulder and struggling to mount.

"Harry!"

He glanced up briefly to see Sadie and Zeke emerging from

the barn, through a dense cloud of black smoke. Sadie was coughing as she led out a horse, and Zeke was on the other side, holding a cloth over the stallion's head.

"Hey!" Zeke shouted toward the man mounting Clipper. "Don't do that! Come back here!"

The man Harry was holding down stirred, and Harry was forced to give all his attention to keeping him prone, but he was aware of Zeke rushing past him and the clatter of hoofbeats growing fainter as Clipper galloped away down the lane.

Within moments, Zeke was at his side with a short piece of rope.

"Here, Mr. Harry, let me tie him with this."

The prisoner was soon trussed and left lying near the well and water trough.

"Where's Sadie?" Harry asked.

"She puttin' Star in the paddock. Come on, Mr. Harry. You think we can do anything about that fire?" Zeke's eyes were bloodshot and streaming tears, and beads of sweat rolled down his face.

Harry looked toward the barn and shook his head. "We might be able to keep it from spreading to the haystacks and your house."

Sadie ran toward them out of the darkness. "The horses are safe. Where are Mitchell and Moe?"

Zeke grimaced. "Mr. Harry got the sergeant. He's tied up over there. That big fella jumped on Clipper and streaked it."

"We need sacks," Harry said. Somehow he felt he ought to greet Sadie and apologize for the way he had left, but there was no time for any of that now.

Sadie cried, "There are two right here. Just dump out the silver. Oh, be careful. I expect my mother's porcelain figurines are in there, too."

Harry and Zeke emptied and soaked the two pillowcases

and began to beat out cinders that flew away from the barn. Sadie filled the two buckets that were handy by the water trough.

"Run to the cabin for more buckets and some blankets," Zeke told her.

❧

Harry and Zeke battled the flames with all their energy. Harry was exhausted, but he kept going, moving things they could salvage away from the burning building and beating back the small blazes that flared up wherever flaming debris landed.

He didn't have time to worry about Sadie but was aware of her running back and forth to the water trough, soaking the wool blankets from Zeke's cabin for them to use in smothering the small fires and hauling more buckets of water from the well.

As they struggled to hold their own against the raging blaze, several horses thundered into the yard. At a shout, Harry looked up to see Pastor Richards jumping down from Pepper's back and Pax clambering down from his perch behind the saddle.

Nearly a dozen men joined him and Zeke as they renewed their efforts to keep the damage to a minimum. The loft full of hay went up in an inferno that drove them back with its stifling heat. Harry watched in awe as the roof turned crimson and collapsed. The men rushed to stamp out the brands that flew throughout the yard and into the paddock. A few small fires even began in the pasture, and men rushed out there with blankets to smother the flames.

At last the blaze was confined to devour what remained of the ruined barn. Harry joined the others at the well. Mr. Ferguson, the innkeeper, poured a bucket of cold, clear water over his blackened head and shoulders. Zeke came toward Harry with another bucketful.

"Here, Mr. Harry. Let me douse you."

Harry let him pour the water over him. It felt good. He shook his head and looked toward the blazing embers of the barn. What a waste! But at least the horses were safe.

❧

Sadie stood back and watched with tears in her eyes as the barn roof caved in, throwing sparks and burning splinters many yards into the air. At least there was no wind to carry the fire farther afield. Her father's old friend, Heinrich Glassbrenner, had arrived with Pax, the pastor, and the other men from town. He had quickly recruited several men to go with him down the nearby path to the river and fill barrels, but it was too late to save anything from the barn.

Sadie's throat hurt as she swallowed back the tears.

Thank You, Lord, she prayed. *Thank You for sending all these friends to help!*

And what about Harry? She couldn't think yet about what his presence meant to her. That was up to him and God.

"Sadie!"

She turned in shock and looked toward the upstairs window.

"Tallie!" Sadie clapped her hand to her mouth. How could she have forgotten about Tallie?

She ran into the house and up the stairs to the door of Tenley's room.

"Tallie, I don't have the key! Are you all right?"

"I'm fine, child. Is everyone out there, too?"

"Yes, I think so, and we got all the horses out. What should I do? The key isn't on this side."

"Send my man in. He'll know how to get me out of here."

Sadie ran down to the yard and found Zeke hauling more buckets of water up out of the well in the barnyard. She reminded him of Tallie's plight, and he quickly located Harry.

"Think we ought to bust the door down, Mr. Harry?"

"Where's the ruffian who locked it?" Harry asked.

Zeke pointed toward a hulk near the paddock fence. They had dragged Mitchell out of the way earlier so the men wouldn't stumble over him when they wet their cloths and filled buckets.

"He be the one," Zeke said, "that fella you rassled with."

Harry strode over to where Mitchell lay and kicked him, but not nearly as hard as Sadie felt like doing.

"Hey!" Harry said. "Where's the key to the room you locked Tallie in?"

Mitchell blinked up at him. "Leave me alone."

Harry grabbed his shirtfront and lifted him a few inches off the grass. "This isn't a good time to make me angry, mister. Where's the key?"

Mitchell was trembling. He looked from Harry over to Sadie. "Don't let him hit me, Miss McEwan!" His brow furrowed, and he stared at her. "How did you get out?"

Zeke leaned down close to Mitchell's face. "God gave her wings, you scoundrel. Now give it up!"

"This isn't my fault," Mitchell screamed as Zeke began rifling his pockets. "I didn't set that fire! Let me go! I can explain everything."

"You'll have plenty of time to do that later," Harry said.

"Here we go!" Zeke straightened and held up the key. He handed it to Sadie. "Tell Tallie I's proud of her and you, and there's about a dozen men here that'll need breakfast once we cool that heap of coals down."

Sadie grabbed the key and ran for the house.

❧

"Tell me ever'thing!" Tallie rushed into Sadie's arms as soon as the door swung open. "Are you hurt? How's my Pax? I thought I seen him once, runnin' to the water trough."

"Pax is fine. No one was hurt, unless you count a few scrapes and bruises."

"Did you get them two no-accounts? What happened to them?"

Sadie frowned and led her toward the stairs. "Harry caught Dan Mitchell, but his friend got away on Clipper. We've probably lost that horse for good. And the barn! Oh, Tallie, it's my fault the barn burned. We're out half our winter's hay, and the buggy, and all the tools and harnesses that were in there!"

"No sense cryin' over it now," Tallie said. "Tell you what. You come wash up and get dressed proper, and we'll give this crew a breakfast like they've only imagined before. Mm-mm! Bacon and flapjacks, eggs, coffee, hash, doughnuts. . .what else?"

Sadie laughed, but she was on the edge of breaking down in tears.

"What do I say to Harry?"

Tallie paused and looked deep into her eyes. "I expect you'll know when the time comes. All right now, put on your corset. Can't let them gentlemen see you like that in the light of day. I'll lace you up; then we'll set to work. The chicken coop didn't get burned, did it?"

"The men let the chickens loose and hauled the coop over near your cabin. We'll have to see how many hens come home to roost when things calm down, but I doubt we'll get many eggs today."

"Well, I've got a couple of dozen in the springhouse. Good thing. I just wish I could have been out there helpin' you! Maybe we could have put that fire out."

"It spread so fast. . . ."

Sadie stopped in the doorway, staring in shock at the shambles of her pretty bedroom. The bedclothes had been torn from the bed, and the mattress was askew. The drawers were open, and her clothing strewn about the room. The jewelry box was gone, as was her toiletry set. Her secretary was tipped over, and her stationery scattered over the rug.

Tallie pushed past her and stood looking at the chaos.

"Well, they made a mess, but they left your clothes." She stepped toward the old spinning wheel in the corner. "Good thing you brought your grandma's old wheel in from the barn last winter."

"Yes," Sadie agreed. "We'd have lost it for sure."

Tallie found Sadie's foundation garment in the corner behind the old spinning wheel and held it out.

"They. . .they touched it."

Tallie grimaced. "Let's not fuss now. This is the time to show what kind of woman you are, missy."

Sadie swallowed and began to unbutton her dress.

nineteen

Dawn was breaking when the men decided it was safe to leave the smoldering ruins and eat breakfast. They washed at the riverbank and came toward the house in a herd. Looking out the window, Sadie realized that more men had joined them from the town, and Mr. Kauffman and his two sons, her nearest neighbors, were among the crowd.

She and Tallie had set up a trestle table outside the lean-to, and they had most of the food laid out already.

"Grab that coffeepot!" Tallie edged past her with a platter of brown sausage and fried potatoes.

They used every plate Sadie could lay her hands on, from her mother's fine china to the battered tin ones Zeke and his sons took on hunting trips. The men stood under the singed trees or sat on the grass that was still green near the house and wolfed down the provisions. Harry mingled with the others, and once Sadie saw him deep in conversation with Pastor Richards.

Wilfred Kauffman came back for seconds and held out his plate, grinning at Sadie. He was the older of Mr. Kauffman's two sons, and it was obvious he was enamored of her. He was a nice enough fellow and would be a good farmer, Sadie supposed. Tenley used to play with him, but she had never liked him much. He was clumsy and a bit dense, she thought. The whole family had the same blond hair and blue eyes, but Wilfred's dull eyes were always watching her, and she didn't like that.

"I'm so glad you're all right, Sadie. We came as soon as we heard."

"Thank you, Wilfred." She placed two more flapjacks on his plate.

Mr. Glassbrenner came back to the table to refill his coffee cup. "Where's your father?" he asked Sadie with a smile. "Not still sick, I hope?"

Sadie gulped. "He. . ."

"He'll be wanting to rebuild that barn," said Mr. Thurber, her friend Elizabeth's father. "You tell him when he's up to it, we'll all come help him clean up the mess and raise a new one."

Mr. Glassbrenner nodded. "He'll be needing supplies. You tell him to come by the mill and see me. We'll work something out."

"Thank you." It was all Sadie could say. She snatched up the empty biscuit platter and dashed into the lean-to.

Harry was just coming out of the house with a pitcher of milk. "Sadie! Are you all right?"

She gasped and stepped aside, out of his path. "Yes, I'm. . ." Suddenly she couldn't stand it a minute longer. "Harry, I'm so sorry! I meant to wait until the others were gone to try to have a word with you, but I can't. The neighbors are all asking about Father, and I don't know what to tell them. I can't go on with this lie. I can't! Not another minute!" She burst into tears, and in her embarrassment she turned away from him, clutching the platter to her breast.

Harry set the pitcher down on the back step and came toward her. She felt his hands on hers, gently prying her fingers loose from the platter. He took it from her and laid it next to the pitcher then drew her toward him.

"Let me handle this for you, Sadie," he whispered, folding his arms around her.

Her breath came in a little gasp. "How can you be so. . . kind? Don't you hate me?"

He sighed and laid his cheek against the top of her head.

"No. I never hated you. Can you forgive me for leaving the way I did?"

"Oh, Harry!" She clung to him for a moment then stepped back, brushing the tears from her cheeks. "I'm sorry. I shouldn't be so forward."

He smiled. "Would you mind if I told the folks about your father? I think it would make things a lot easier for you."

"Would you?"

"Yes. And as to the rest of it, well, perhaps we can talk again later."

She made herself meet his steady gaze. His brown eyes were clear and bright, and their tender expression made her heart leap. She nodded. "I'd like that."

He picked up the milk pitcher and stepped outside the lean-to. Sadie abandoned the platter and went to stand near Tallie behind the table.

"Folks!" Harry shouted, raising his hand, and the chattering stopped. "A few of you know me," he said, "but for those who don't, I'm Harry Cooper, a friend of the McEwan family."

Sadie's breath went out of her in a puff. He wasn't angry. He was representing himself to her neighbors as a friend. *Thank You, Lord!* she breathed. Even if he left now and never came back, she was content. But she realized she hoped fiercely that he wouldn't go. Not now, not until things were settled between them. *We can talk again later,* he'd said. Sadie seized the joy that prospect brought her.

"Several of you have inquired about Oliver McEwan today," Harry said, and all the men gathered closer, eager to listen.

Sadie glanced at Tallie. Pax came and stood between them, and Tallie placed her hand on the boy's shoulder. "Mr. Harry's goin' to straighten things out," Tallie whispered, and Sadie nodded.

"It grieves me to have to give you the news," Harry said, "but in order to spare Miss McEwan the pain of doing so, let me tell you that Oliver McEwan has passed away." A murmur ran through the crowd, and Harry went on. "There's been a lot of confusion here, with the house being robbed and the fire, but I'm certain Oliver would be glad to know how many of his friends are here to help his family in this time of need. Miss McEwan hasn't had a chance to make arrangements yet, but I'm sure the word will get around to all of you soon, and perhaps a small memorial service will be held."

He glanced around and found her, a question in his dark eyes. Sadie nodded and pressed her lips together.

As the men stood staring at Harry, hoofbeats sounded along the road, growing louder, and a lone horse trotted up the driveway.

They all stared in silence at the empty saddle as Clipper entered the yard and stopped, shaking his head and eyeing the smoking rubble of the barn in confusion.

"Isn't that your father's stallion?" Mr. Kauffman called to Sadie.

"Yes, it is. One of the robbers rode off on him before you got here."

"That must be the man who raced past us when we came to the lane," Pastor Richards said. "We called out to him, but he didn't stop."

Sadie looked to Harry. He'd left his spot and was walking toward Clipper.

"That hoss is an ornery one," Zeke said. "Let me get him, Mr. Harry." He walked toward the stallion, passing Harry, and held out half a biscuit. "Here now, fella. You're home now."

Clipper stretched his neck out and delicately took the biscuit with his lips. Zeke snatched the trailing reins, and the horse immediately threw his head back and tried to pull away.

"Here now." Zeke spoke softly to him until Clipper let him stroke his neck. He led the horse to the hitching rail near the house and unsaddled him. Harry followed and ran his hand down Clipper's sweaty shoulder.

"I don't know as we want to turn him into the pasture, Mr. Harry," Zeke said. "He's been known to jump a fence or two. The small paddock will hold him, but I've got Star in there. Wouldn't want two stallions in such a small pen."

Harry nodded. "I guess we'll have to tie him up someplace until we sort things out, Zeke." He turned and looked toward the barn. "We've got a lot of work to do."

Zeke smiled. "Yes, suh!"

The men had gone back to eating and talking to each other. Harry shot a sidelong glance at Sadie, and her pulse accelerated. He smiled, and she tried to smile back, wanting him to know how much she appreciated all he had done. But her lips trembled. Her love for him surged up, taking her breath away.

She didn't deserve Harry Cooper! He was too fine for her. She'd deceived him all that time, and then she'd brought this new calamity on them all by letting Dan Mitchell in the house. And she had burned the barn down to save a little money and a few trinkets! Something in the far reaches of her mind told her that wasn't accurate. She'd been trying to save Zeke, too, when she'd thrown that horseshoe and caused the fire, but she couldn't quite piece it together and make sense of it. She was so tired!

She hurried in through the front door and up the stairs.

❧

"You're needed down below, Miss Sadie."

Sadie wiped her eyes, rolled to the edge of the bed, and sat up. "I'm sorry, Tallie. I shouldn't have left you alone with all that work."

Tallie shrugged. "I was hopin' you'd rest, but I see you been feelin' sorry for yourself instead."

"I'll come now and help you clean up."

"We got all day to clean up. Most of them men are gone.

They took that thief Mitchell with them. But they's two gen'lemen waitin' in the parlor to see you."

Sadie swallowed. Her throat still hurt, and the smell of smoke was still in her nostrils. "Two?"

"Uh-huh. Pastor Richards and Mr. Harry."

Sadie stood up. Her legs didn't feel strong enough to hold her, and she grabbed the corner post of the bed.

"Please tell them I'll be there shortly."

Tallie's expression softened. "Let me help you freshen up a little, child."

Sadie looked in the mirror. Although Tallie had helped her scrub away the soot earlier, her face was still dirty with smudges where her tears had smeared. Her eyes were red from the smoke and weeping, and the skin beneath them was puffy.

She washed her face, patting the cool, wet cloth against her swollen eyelids. Then Tallie insisted she sit down and let her comb out her matted hair.

"Mr. Kauffman and Mr. Thurber both say they'll come over tomorrow to help Zeke and Mr. Harry, and their wives will send some food."

"That's kind of them," Sadie said.

At last Tallie stood back and said, "There. You still smell like smoke, but I expect they'll understand."

❧

Harry stood at the side parlor window, carefully removing the shards of glass from the frame with his handkerchief. At least Tallie hadn't splintered the sash. Harry had spotted the broken window when Tallie asked him and Pastor Richards to wait in there for Sadie, apologizing for the state of the room. Harry thought there might be an extra pane left in the lean-to. He'd check on it later. Meanwhile Pastor Richards gathered scattered papers and accessories from the floor, returning them to the oak rolltop desk.

Sadie came to the doorway, and Harry turned toward her. She had been weeping, and he didn't blame her. He wished he could take her into his arms again, but with Pastor Richards present, he couldn't do that. He smiled at her.

"Sadie, I'm so sorry you had to go through all this."

The pastor stepped forward and took Sadie's hand in his. "Yes, my dear. Mr. Cooper has explained some things to me, and I must tell you how my heart aches for you. You've been a very brave girl."

"No," she said, blinking back her tears. "I wasn't brave at all, Pastor. I was a coward, and so I did the cowardly thing. I let Harry think. . ." She pulled in a deep breath then looked directly at Harry. "I let him think Papa was alive, and that was a lie."

"Sit down, Sadie, dear," said the pastor. "From what I hear, most of this deception was Zeke's doing, not yours."

She shook her head. "It may have started with Zeke, but I let it go on. I could have stopped it at the very beginning, but I didn't. And after a while I joined in it. Harry begged me to tell him what was wrong, but I wouldn't." She looked down at her hands and sighed. "I'm so sorry, Harry."

"I told you, Sadie—that's forgiven."

Sadie pulled her handkerchief out of her sleeve and wiped her eyes.

Pastor Richards cleared his throat. "Perhaps when you feel better, you could show me your father's grave."

"Yes, of course." She sniffed. "We could go out there now, if you wish."

Harry hung back, letting Richards walk with Sadie, and followed them into the front hall.

"I think Mr. Cooper's suggestion is a good one," the pastor said. "If you'd like, we can have a brief graveside service. Perhaps on Wednesday. There would be no need to tell folks how long your father's been gone."

Sadie sobbed and put her handkerchief to her lips for a moment then whispered, "Thank you, sir. I'd like that."

They stepped outside and were heading for the path that led to the burial plot when once more a horse came up the drive. Zeke came from the lean-to, looking toward the approaching horse.

Harry recognized the rider as Mr. Ferguson.

"We found that fellow!" the innkeeper shouted.

Sadie, Harry, Zeke, and Mr. Richards walked toward him, and Ferguson dismounted.

"You found the second robber?" Harry asked.

"Yes, a great big man with a scar." He touched his left cheek.

Sadie said, "That's Moe, the one who rode off on Clipper. I'm sure of it."

"What happened?" Harry asked.

"He was lying in the road beside the bridge between here and town. I beg your pardon for being indelicate, Miss McEwan, but. . .well, his neck's broken. Looks like the horse threw him."

"Don't surprise me none," Zeke said. "That hoss would buck if the least little thing hit him back of the saddle."

"They're taking him into town in Glassbrenner's wagon," Mr. Ferguson said. "Oh, and these were in his pockets, Miss McEwan. We thought perhaps. . ."

He held out a wad of folded bills and a gold pocket watch. Sadie stared down at them. "The watch is my father's. There was some money taken, too."

Ferguson pressed the items into her hand. "I'll be going now. See you later, Mr. Cooper. Breakfast for your dinner tonight?"

Harry said, "Oh, well, I may be dining here this evening." He looked at Sadie with a question in his eyes.

"Please do," she said.

"You'd best stay right here, Mr. Harry," said Zeke. "Iffen you want, I can go get your things from in town."

Ferguson laughed as he mounted his horse. "You want your stuff, Mr. Cooper? Because I can still rent your room out. Big wedding tomorrow, right, Parson?"

Pastor Richards nodded. "Yes, Sarah Murray and John Hofstead."

Harry hesitated. "Well. . ." He glanced at Sadie again, and to his consternation, felt his face flushing.

"Please stay, Harry," she said, not looking at him, in a voice so low only he could hear her.

It was all he needed. "All right then, Zeke. I'd appreciate it if you'd do that for me."

Zeke's grin made everything seem right again. "Yes, suh, Mr. Harry! I'd be pleasured to do that thing! I'll get me a horse to ride and be back in an hour with your things from the inn." He turned and trotted toward the pasture gate.

Harry walked with Sadie and Pastor Richards as far as the fence surrounding the burial ground. He left them there together and walked on to the river, taking his time, and went along the bank to the place where the McEwans had a boat landing. He circled back by another path to the barnyard and stood looking at the remains of the barn. Here and there a wisp of smoke escaped the charred ruins. Harry tried to figure when they could begin the cleanup and how long it would take to get the materials and raise the new barn. If all the neighbors pitched in, they ought to be able to do it before winter set in.

The circuit rider and Sadie came back from the graveyard, and Sadie slipped into the big house through the lean-to. Mr. Richards joined Harry in the barnyard.

"Is she all right?" Harry asked.

"She's been through a great deal," the parson replied. "She's a strong woman, though. With loved ones to support her, I'm sure she'll get through this."

Harry nodded. "Did she mention how frightened she was of losing her home?"

"Yes. I think that can be straightened out. She told me her father left the estate to Tenley, but of course he predeceased Oliver. That might complicate things, but I offered to look into it for her."

"That's good of you, sir."

Richards shrugged. "I do many things to help my flock. I often meet Judge Ryerton in my travels. Our circuits intersect every couple of months, you see. The next time I see him, which I calculate will be soon, I'll make a discreet inquiry on Miss McEwan's behalf."

"Thank you," Harry said. "If she needs to go into town and sign papers or anything like that, I'll take her."

"It might help if she could find her father's will," the pastor said. "Lawyers like to see a document. They'd rather not take your word for something like that."

Harry frowned. "There must be a will. She was certain the property was left in her brother's name."

"She says there is, but she's not sure exactly where it is. It may be in her father's room or in his desk, but things are in quite a jumble now. It may have been misplaced. I advised her to ask Tallie if she knows about it, since Tallie usually does the cleaning."

It was nearly noon, and Harry turned toward the house. They walked to the back door, and Harry showed Pastor Richards where he could wash in the lean-to. As they were finishing, Tallie looked out the kitchen door.

"Mr. Harry, you ought to know better than to have comp'ny wash out here," she said, her eyebrows almost meeting in a frown.

"I'm sorry," Harry told her. "I've gotten used to it, and I don't stand on ceremony here."

"Well," Tallie said, nodding, "that's right. You's family now.

But the preacher is another story."

Mr. Richards laughed. "I'm all right, Tallie. You don't have to give me a fancy china basin to wash in."

"Well, at least I can get you a fresh towel." Tallie disappeared for a moment, and the pastor waited with his hands dripping over the tin washbasin. When she reappeared with a clean towel, he took it with a smile.

"Thank you. You make a man feel right at home."

"Well, now, you just get around to the front door, both of you," she replied. "I sent Miss Sadie into the dinin' room, and she'll sit down with you now."

Harry glanced at the pastor. Richards was holding his smile in check. They walked around to the front of the house, and Harry led the minister through the hall and into the dining room.

Sadie whirled from the window as they entered. Her cheeks flushed as she met Harry's gaze.

"I'm so glad you could both join me for luncheon," she murmured. "Mr. Cooper, will you sit here, please?" She touched the back of the chair at the head of the table.

Harry looked at her in surprise. That was her father's place, he knew, and in all the time since he had returned to the Spinning Wheel Farm in September, no one had sat in that chair.

She was waiting for his response, he realized. He nodded and stepped forward.

"Thank you," she whispered. "And you here, Pastor, across from me, if you don't mind."

Harry pulled out the chair in which Sadie customarily sat. Her flush was pronounced as she took her seat. Harry sat down in Oliver's chair. Sadie wasn't looking at him. Instead, she held the circuit rider's gaze.

"And, Pastor, if you would be so kind as to offer grace?"

They bowed their heads, and as the pastor spoke, Harry

breathed carefully. Things would work out. They had to.

Please, Lord, he prayed silently, *show me what to do next.* Even with his eyes closed, he could feel Sadie's energy. The pastor's voice went on at length, seeking God's blessing on Sadie and her dependents. Harry exhaled and sent up another prayer. *Let her love me, Lord, even a tenth as much as I love her. And let her allow me to take care of her.*

At Richards's amen, Harry opened his eyes. Sadie glanced at him, and he smiled. She smiled back with a hopeful gladness that spoke to Harry's heart.

twenty

"Careful now." Sadie took her mother's china figurines from Tallie's hands and turned to place them with care on the mantelpiece.

"At least we got back all your things." Tallie ran her dust rag over the windowsill and the frames of the paintings.

"Yes," said Sadie. "The barn is the biggest loss. I'm afraid the buggy and harness will be costly. We may have to wait awhile to replace them."

"Well, Mr. Harry says we can get the lumber in and have a new barn raised before long." Tallie began to hum as she plumped the cushions on the settee.

Sadie bit her lip. She wasn't sure how to take Harry's actions. Apparently he and Zeke were already deep into their plans for a community barn raising. Did that mean he would stay here for several more weeks? They definitely needed to discuss some things.

Zeke had insisted on carrying Harry's luggage to Tenley's bedroom. Sadie had consented to this arrangement on condition that Tallie sleep in the little room off the kitchen. To her surprise, neither Tallie nor Zeke had objected this time.

After the pastor left, Harry and Zeke had gone out to poke around the ruins of the barn, and Sadie didn't expect to see Harry again until suppertime. She and Tallie had begun to clean up the parlor in earnest. Nothing seemed to be missing or broken. Harry had already cleaned up the broken glass from the window and replaced the pane. How many things had he done for her today? From the moment he'd galloped into the yard and leaped on Dan Mitchell, he had gone about making things right at the McEwan farm. Sadie would never be able to express her gratitude to its full extent.

As if her thoughts had drawn him, Harry appeared in the parlor doorway. His endearing smile warmed her, and she marveled that she felt so contented when only a few hours ago she'd been in turmoil.

"I wanted to tell you, Zeke and I think we can salvage a lot of hardware from the barn."

"Praise the Lawd," Tallie said.

Sadie smiled. "Yes, that will be a savings for us."

Harry nodded. "The only saddle that survived is the one Pax had on Clipper, but at least we have that one saddle and bridle. Oh, and we have some boards Zeke had stored behind the chicken coop. We thought we'd knock together a few benches for seating at the memorial service on Wednesday."

"Do you think many people will come?" Sadie asked.

"Judging by the turnout last night, I wouldn't be surprised if quite a few came, and the pastor said he'll spread the word in town. If the weather is fine, you can hold it outside near the graveyard."

Sadie nodded, looking around at the parlor. "If it rains, I suppose we'll have it in here."

"Oh, we'd best do some baking tomorrow!" Tallie closed her eyes and smiled.

"Folks will bring food, won't they?" Sadie asked.

"Yes, they surely will, but the dainties they'll talk about most will come right out of our kitchen."

Sadie laughed. "Careful, Tallie. You're getting mighty proud of your cooking."

"With good reason," Harry said with a grin. "Now don't you ladies wear yourselves out with cooking and cleaning."

"Two of the neighbor ladies are comin' tomorrow to help us, and my Ephraim's wife, Dulcy," Tallie assured him. "I sent Pax over to tell Ephraim what happened, and Dulcy said she'll come right after breakfast and bring her big girl, too."

"Good," said Harry. "I'm glad you'll have some help."

"They's soot and ashes everywhere," Tallie said. "It'll take us a week to get everything clean, but we'll make sure this parlor and the dining room sparkle on Wednesday for Mr. Oliver's service." She stooped and picked up an envelope that had slid along the floor and was almost hidden under the settee.

Harry looked toward Tallie then took a step nearer Sadie. "May I count on having some time alone with you this evening?"

Sadie drew in a slow breath, savoring the moment. "Yes, Harry."

He smiled and reached to give her hand a squeeze, and she thought her heart would burst.

"Oh, glory, glory!" Tallie shrieked. "Praise the Lawd! Praise the Lawd!"

"What is it?" Sadie asked.

Tallie held out the envelope she had retrieved. "This be what you said to look for, Mr. Harry. It's that paper Mr. Oliver signed when Mr. Tenley went away with the army. He had me and Zeke put our marks to it."

Sadie's hand trembled as she reached for it and took the document from the envelope. She had never seen it, but she knew at once what it was. "She's right, Harry. It's Papa's will." She sat down in one of the cherry side chairs, feeling a bit unsteady. "Would you mind reading it?"

She held it out to him, and Harry took it, his face full of compassion.

"If you're sure you want me to."

"Yes! Waiting any longer won't do us any good."

Tallie clasped her hands at her breast and watched as he glanced over the sheet then separated it from a second one and stood staring at it, frowning.

"What is it?" Sadie asked.

Harry looked up. "It's. . .Sadie, did you know your brother made a will?"

"I. . .no." She caught her breath and turned to Tallie. "Did you know of such a thing, Tallie?"

Tallie shook her head. "I never."

Harry nodded slowly, looking at the papers again. "Well, this first sheet is Mr. McEwan's will all right, and it's as you said, Sadie. He's left his entire estate to his son, with the provision that Tenley would give you tenancy here at the farm as long as you want it." He slid that paper behind the other. "This second sheet appears to be a will that Tenley made when he joined the army. It's witnessed by a private and a corporal. Apparently he entrusted it to your father, and Mr. McEwan placed it in the envelope with his own document."

Sadie felt tears flooding her eyes once more. "Papa never told me."

Tallie was also weeping openly, and she mopped her eyes with her apron.

Harry stepped closer to Sadie and placed his warm hand on her shoulder. "Sadie, dearest, your brother left his worldly goods to you."

"Bless that boy," Tallie cried. "Oh, Mr. Harry, does that mean Miss Sadie gets to keep her home?"

"I think it does."

"Glory, glory! Thank You, Lawd!"

Sadie couldn't help but smile. "Tallie, if you'd like to go and tell Zeke. . ."

"Yes'm, I'll do just that!" Tallie rushed out the doorway.

Sadie sniffed and blinked a couple of times then wiped her cheeks with her handkerchief. "What do I do now, Harry?"

"Pastor Richards mentioned a judge who comes around on a circuit."

She nodded. "Judge Ryerton. He's dined here before."

"Well, Pastor Richards will be here Wednesday for the memorial service. Perhaps he'll advise you on the best way to contact the justice and take care of this. I confess, I'm not up on legal matters, but probably these will go through probate court."

Sadie sighed. "Papa never said a word, even after we heard Tenley was dead. But perhaps he was waiting for Judge Ryerton to come around again."

"I'm not an expert," Harry said, "but God has allowed us to find these papers, and I think what it says here should comfort you."

"It does." She stood and looked at him, managing a trembling smile. "So does your presence, Harry."

He leaned toward her and brushed her lips with a soft kiss then stepped back as they heard Tallie's footsteps in the hallway.

❧

On Wednesday Sadie sat beside Harry on a wooden bench just outside the graveyard fence. Forty neighbors and friends filled the benches behind them, and more than a dozen men stood at the back. Zeke, Tallie, Pax, Ephraim, Dulcy, and their children stood to one side. Pastor Richards led them in hymns of praise to God then spoke with affection and respect for Oliver McEwan's life.

The late October breeze was cool but not bone chilling. Zeke and his sons had gathered late blooms from the flower beds and heaped them over Oliver McEwan's grave. No one asked how long he had been buried.

At Sadie's request the pastor included Tenley in the memorial. Her brother's body was buried outside Mexico City and would remain there, but Sadie had decided to have a small stone prepared in Tenley's memory when she had her father's done and have it placed it between the graves of their parents.

Her sorrow made a fresh assault on her as she listened, and she soaked both the handkerchiefs she'd stowed in her pockets. Harry's eyes were moist, too, as he reached over to squeeze her hand. She clung to him, and he held her hand through the closing prayer.

The neighbors lingered to commiserate with Sadie over strong tea and luncheon. The women of the neighborhood had contributed enough food to provision a small army. Tallie's roasted haunch of beef and berry pies took pride of place on the dining room table. Guests filed through and filled the plates loaned for the occasion by the women of the neighborhood then found places to sit in the parlor, on the porch, or on benches the men had brought up from the cemetery to the dooryard. Harry never left Sadie's side.

The sun was falling over the mountains to the west before the guests left. Elizabeth Thurber and her mother lingered to help with the cleanup while Mr. Thurber engaged Harry and Pastor Richards in conversation.

"You didn't tell me about your beau," Elizabeth whispered to Sadie as they cleared the table.

"My. . .you mean Harry?"

"He's splendid!" Elizabeth picked up two pie tins. "Poor Wilfred was despondent. Did you notice?"

"No," Sadie admitted.

"Of course not. You weren't thinking about things like that today." Elizabeth gave her a squeeze. "I love you, Sadie. I'm sorry about your father."

"Thank you." Sadie hugged her back. "You and your family are good friends."

"Well, if you need anything or you just want to have a good talk, ride over and see me."

"I will."

At last Elizabeth's family drove away in their wagon, with Mr. Thurber assuring Harry he would be back with his farm wagon on Saturday to help cut some logs to make beams for the new barn. Pastor Richards declined supper and left on horseback, promising Sadie a speedy resolution to her legal situation. Ephraim and his family were the only ones remaining, and they were staying for a supper of leftovers in the kitchen with Zeke, Tallie, and Pax.

Sadie tried to enter the kitchen to help with the meal preparation, but Dulcy shooed her away, so she hastened upstairs. She'd been in her room only minutes when Tallie knocked on her door.

"I brung you some warm water," Tallie said, carrying in a steaming pitcher.

"Thank you. I just want to wash up and fix my hair before dinner. I'm rather windblown, I'm afraid."

"Let me help you, child."

Tallie reached to unbutton Sadie's black dress, but Sadie shook her head. "I'm going to wear this tonight."

Tallie frowned. "Seems to me you ought to spruce up a bit for Mr. Harry after all he's done for us."

Sadie felt the blood rush to her cheeks. "Harry doesn't expect me to try to dazzle him."

"All the better," Tallie said. "Surprise him. If you put on that green velvet dress, he'll know you did it just for him."

Sadie bit her lip. "Today was my father's funeral," she whispered.

Tallie nodded. "I know it, and Mr. Harry knows it. Your papa wouldn't want you to mope around in black, and you know it. Why, if he was here he'd say, Pretty up for your guest tonight, Sadie, and be a good hostess like your mama used to be. Then git up at dawn and go ride one of them hosses with Mr. Harry."

Sadie smiled. "He wouldn't really say that."

"Oh, wouldn't he just? He liked Mr. Harry. You know he did." Tallie opened the wardrobe and lifted the heavy green gown out. "This is what we been prayin' for. The man you love is downstairs waiting."

Sadie closed her eyes for an instant, seeking guidance. She went to Tallie and took the hanger from her hands, returning the gown to the wardrobe. "I'll save it for another evening, Tallie. Tonight I just need to be. . .plain Sadie."

Harry talked quietly during dinner, explaining to her his plan to help Zeke and the neighbors build a new barn.

"It will be smaller than the old one, but it will get you through the winter," he said. "If we can put it up and get the roof on within two weeks, I think I can get to Kentucky while the mountains are still passable."

She nodded, fighting the lump that was forming in her throat. Harry was leaving again. She had expected it, but it hurt.

"Do you think you'll be all right for a while if I do that?" he asked.

"I. . .yes. We'll be fine, Harry. You'll want to get the mares home as quickly as possible."

His eyes widened. "Well, no, I. . .thought I'd leave them here. If it's all right with you."

Tallie removed their plates, frowning but silent.

Sadie looked up at Harry. "I don't understand."

He took a breath then glanced toward Tallie's retreating figure. "Sadie, could we. . .perhaps we could go into the parlor now."

"You don't want dessert?"

"No, I'm fine, and I need to speak to you alone."

She swallowed hard. Tallie returned from the kitchen carrying two dessert plates.

"Please bring Mr. Harry's coffee into the parlor," Sadie said, rising.

Tallie blinked at her in astonishment then turned to Harry. "I've got pecan pie, Mr. Harry."

"Oh, Tallie, that sounds wonderful, but I ate so much after the funeral that I think I'd better pass on the pie tonight. Will you save me a piece for tomorrow?"

" 'Course I will. Go on now."

Harry held his hand out to Sadie, and she took it. She went with him into the parlor and sat down on the settee, unable to meet Harry's burning gaze.

"Sadie, dearest," he said, sitting down beside her, "I hope you understand. I need to go back to Kentucky, just for a short time. I don't want to leave you in a mess, so I'll wait until we have the new barn up, but. . ."

Sadie sat speechless, staring at him, and Harry winced.

"I'm coming at this backward, aren't I?" he asked.

"Well. . ." She wasn't sure how to respond so she waited, her heart hammering.

Harry slid off the settee to one knee and reached for her hands. "I love you, Sadie."

She could breathe then. She squeezed his hands and tried to speak, but nothing came out, and tears were threatening her again.

He looked at her with his tender, purposeful brown eyes. "Will you marry me?"

She gasped. "Oh, Harry, do you mean it? I've been so wicked!"

"No. Don't think that."

"But I do! And you have your farm in Kentucky."

"Yes, but that's what I was going to tell you. If you'll be my wife, we can go there if you want and build a new farm, or we can stay here. Sadie, I know you love this place, and it's your home. I'd be willing to sell my land in Kentucky and move here. A neighbor out there would love to have it. But I don't want you to think I'm only doing this because of the land. If the judge told us tomorrow you couldn't keep this place, it wouldn't make any difference to me. I love you so much that it doesn't matter to me where we live, just so you'll be happy." He stopped and bit his lower lip. "Does that make sense to you?"

She smiled, wishing she could banish the tears in her eyes. "Yes, Harry. It makes perfect sense. I'd like to stay here and get the farm back to how it was when Papa ran it. That may take awhile, though, with this setback."

He shook his head. "Darling, I'd be happy to invest in this place. In the spring we can be married, and we'll build a bigger barn then. And if that stud colt of yours doesn't turn out the way we want, we can ride over to Richmond together and look for another one, and. . ."

Sadie felt her cheeks go scarlet, but she couldn't make herself look away from his eager face.

"Sorry," Harry said. "I was getting a bit carried away there, but you understand."

"Yes. Yes, I do."

"Does that mean. . .you'll marry me?"

"Yes, Harry. Nothing would make me happier."

He smiled and whispered, "Thank you! Whatever it takes, Sadie, I'm sure we can make a go of it together."

"Are you certain you want to give up your dream in Kentucky?"

"Yes. I have a new dream now, and you're in the center of it."

He sat beside her on the settee once more and pulled her into his arms. Sadie thrilled at his touch. She closed her eyes as his lips met hers, losing herself in the dream of their future.

Harry held her for a long moment, with her head nestled over his heart.

"Praise the Lawd!"

Sadie's eyes flew open, and she sat straighter, pulling away from him as Tallie entered the room with Harry's coffee cup on a tray.

He laughed. "Thank you, Tallie. You can tell Zeke to be up bright and early, and we'll get to work on the barn. I need to finish it quickly so I can get to Kentucky before the snow flies."

"I'll do that, Mr. Harry, but. . .you are coming back, aren't you? 'Cause iffen you're not. . ." Tallie threw a meaningful glance at Sadie.

"You don't have to worry about your mistress," Harry assured her. "Miss Sadie is going to become Mrs. Cooper as soon as I return from my trip to sell my farm in Kentucky."

"Glory, glory!" Tallie shouted. She set the tray down and bustled toward the kitchen.

Sadie smiled at Harry. "You'd better relax and enjoy your coffee while you can. When Zeke hears the news, he'll want to talk everything over with you and make plans."

"Zeke can wait." Harry drew her into his arms again, ignoring his coffee.

epilogue

May 1849

Sadie held her hoops in and stepped carefully through her bedroom doorway into the hall. Dulcy followed, holding up the hem of her white satin skirt in the back. Elizabeth Thurber came toward them from the stairs.

"Oh, Sadie, you look marvelous!"

"So do you." Sadie hugged Elizabeth then stood back to admire her friend's frothy apricot gown. Tallie and Dulcy fussed about her.

"Careful now, girl. You mussin' up your bride's dress." Tallie arranged the folds of Sadie's skirt while Dulcy smoothed the lacy veil.

"Is everyone ready?" Sadie asked, a little breathless.

"I'm ready, and the minister's ready," Elizabeth laughed, "but if you mean Harry, yes, he's more than ready. Papa said he's been pacing like a panther in a cage this last half hour."

Sadie smiled. Harry had returned from Kentucky three weeks ago and had made no secret of his anticipation of the wedding day.

She and Elizabeth slowly descended the stairs. Mr. Thurber met them in the lower hall, outside the parlor door.

"You look lovely, my dear," he said. "Are you ready?"

"Yes, sir. Thank you for standing in for Papa."

Mr. Thurber stooped and kissed Sadie's cheek. "I'm honored. Oliver was a good man and a good friend."

Tallie lowered the veil over Sadie's face then slipped away with Dulcy to squeeze into the far corner of the parlor with the rest of their family.

Elizabeth kissed Sadie and went through the door. Sadie found herself gripping Mr. Thurber's arm and stepping forward. The Thurbers, the Kauffmans, the Glassbrenners, and several other neighbors were packed into the room, and Zeke's family beamed at her from the corners. Harry stood before the fireplace where large vases of apple blossoms graced the mantelpiece. Clara Glassbrenner played softly on her dulcimer. Everyone was smiling, but Sadie had eyes only for Harry. As she walked with Mr. Thurber between the rows of guests and drew closer to Harry, she could see love radiating from his eyes. She stood trembling as Pastor Richards welcomed the people, and Harry's warm smile calmed her. At last she was able to place her hand in his and begin their new life together.

A Letter To Our Readers

Dear Reader:
In order that we might better contribute to your reading enjoyment, we would appreciate your taking a few minutes to respond to the following questions. We welcome your comments and read each form and letter we receive. When completed, please return to the following:

Fiction Editor
Heartsong Presents
PO Box 719
Uhrichsville, Ohio 44683

1. Did you enjoy reading *Weaving a Future* by Susan Page Davis?
   ❑ Very much! I would like to see more books by this author!
   ❑ Moderately. I would have enjoyed it more if
   ____
   ____
   ____

2. Are you a member of **Heartsong Presents**? ❑ Yes ❑ No
   If no, where did you purchase this book? ______________
   ____

3. How would you rate, on a scale from 1 (poor) to 5 (superior), the cover design? ______________

4. On a scale from 1 (poor) to 10 (superior), please rate the following elements.

____ Heroine	____ Plot
____ Hero	____ Inspirational theme
____ Setting	____ Secondary characters

5. These characters were special because? ________________

____

____

6. How has this book inspired your life? ________________

____

____

7. What settings would you like to see covered in future **Heartsong Presents** books? ________________

____

____

8. What are some inspirational themes you would like to see treated in future books? ________________

____

____

9. Would you be interested in reading other **Heartsong Presents** titles? ❑ Yes ❑ No

10. Please check your age range:

❑ Under 18	❑ 18-24
❑ 25-34	❑ 35-45
❑ 46-55	❑ Over 55

Name ____

Occupation ____________________________________

Address ______________________________________

City, State, Zip _________________________________